GUIDEPOSTS

CHURCH CHOIR
MYSTERIES™

The Regrettable Rumors

Eileen M. Berger

Guideposts®

CARMEL, NEW YORK 10512

www.guidepostsbooks.com

www.guidepostsbooks.com
Guideposts Books & Inspirational Media Division
Series Editor: Michele Slung
Cover art by Stephen Gardner & Edgar Jerins
Cover design by Wendy Bass
Interior design by José R. Fonfrias
Interior cat illustrations by Viqui Maggio
Typeset by Composition Technologies, Inc.
Printed in the United States of America

This novel is lovingly dedicated to
the wonderful people in my own
north-central Pennsylvania community who serve or served
every bit as selflessly and generously
as do our Willow Bend friends.
Among these are:
Drs. Callenberger, Sorber, Dilcher, Smaha and Bennett,
Chief of Police Joe Walker,
Mayor Pauline Montgomery,
editor Dave Troisi,
organists/choir directors—
Linda Leonard and Arlene Strausser,
the members of our East Lycoming ministerium,
and so many, many others too numerous to mention.

Acknowledgments

WHAT A PRIVILEGE and joy it has been to get to know and to work with the wonderful people at Guideposts Books and Inspirational Media Division! They are excellent at their profession, but are also approachable and helpful in other ways—including having lifted up members of my family in their prayers.

Thank you to all of them, especially Elizabeth Kramer Gold, editor par excellence, as well as Michele Slung, Stephanie Castillo Samoy and Brigitte Weeks for their skill, patience and know-how, and for giving me the opportunity to write this, my fifth "Church Choir Mysteries" novel.

THE AIR HAD BEEN CRISP and invigorating when Gracie Parks and her large orange cat Gooseberry started on their walk, but by now, 7:30 A.M., she'd slipped out of her windbreaker and was carrying it over her arm as they entered Abe's Deli.

"Welcome!" The pair was greeted warmly by Abe Wasserman, the proprietor, as he carried a plate with four bagels toward the only occupied table. "Sit anywhere, Gracie! I'll be with you in a moment."

"We're not in a hurry." Taking one of the high red vinyl seats at the counter, she smiled at the other two men as well. "Isn't this a perfect day?"

Harvey Smith looked a little surprised as he glanced at her and her cat, then quickly away. Tony Randolph, however, nodded in acknowledgment. "Yeah. Just right."

Then Abe had come back, and she asked, "Any blueberry bagels? We had a great walk."

"Right from the oven, not over ten minutes ago."

"Well, as usual, I'm going to justify buying a half-dozen by telling myself Uncle Miltie will enjoy them immensely."

"He will." Her friend grinned at the familiar rationalization. "And for you, right now, some tea or coffee?"

"Not this morning." She glanced at her watch. "I promised to take a friend to a doctor's appointment, and by the time I get home and take my shower, it will be time to get going again."

Gooseberry obviously was ready for a change of scenery and was on his way toward the door before Gracie turned on the stool. He knew cat food wasn't on the menu at the deli, though a tidbit of smoked fish sometimes did come his way when he meowed loudly enough at Abe.

Gracie's farewell included all three men as she followed her cat. "Have a good day!" she called.

It didn't surprise her, however, when only Abe responded, "You, too, Gracie!"

It had seemed odd to find Tony and Harvey here together. Of course their families had long histories in Willow Bend, so they'd known one another all their lives. However, they'd run against one another for the position of mayor two different times, and some of their election campaigning had become not only personal, but downright nasty!

And now they were both running again! She sighed, recalling the visit she'd received ten days before from two concerned citizens trying to get her to enter the race. Gracie Lynn Parks, ace politico? Not a chance!

Therefore, she'd assured them that she had no interest whatsoever in their plan.

It wasn't that she didn't love Willow Bend, for it had been her favorite place in the entire world ever since she'd come here as a bride many years ago. And it wasn't that she didn't want to devote all the time she knew such a campaign would entail—not to mention serving in office if she actually won. Hadn't she been married to Elmo Parks through his two terms as mayor?

But she already served the community in the best way she possibly could—by being, simply, herself. She didn't need—or want—a title.

She'd never even mentioned these feelers to her uncle, George Morgan, otherwise known as Uncle Miltie. Gracie sometimes wondered what life would be like had he not come to live with her after they'd both found themselves widowed. Life with this octogenarian was almost always merry—unless his osteoarthritis was really acting up. Still, his good humor was pretty constant, as long as one could tolerate the corny jokes that reminded folks of the old-time comedian, Milton Berle, which had earned him his nickname. She doubted that most people even realized *Miltie* wasn't his real name.

It was while she and Uncle Miltie were eating lunch that she thought to say, "You'll never guess who was at Abe's when I got there."

He looked up from pouring a small amount of molasses on a large cornbread muffin. "In that case, I pass."

"Tony and Harvey! I thought they hated each other."

"*Hmmm.*" He took a big bite and wiped syrup off his upper lip as he chewed and swallowed. "Must be something going on to get those two even speaking, much less eating breakfast together."

"That was my reaction, too."

"Were they pleasant? I assume they must have been talking to one another, but did they say anything to you?"

"Well, Tony acknowledged as how it was a nice day, but Harvey kept mum. Eating at Abe's usually makes even the biggest curmudgeons in town more sociable."

Her uncle reached for the cabbage salad. "I'm not gonna lose sleep over it."

"I might if I were the only person they didn't like, but since I figure I've got lots of good company. . . ."

"You know, I've always wondered what ever happened to Harvey's son Martin. He was around town when I first got here, and then he kind of disappeared. He seemed a little mixed-up, but he was polite to us older guys when he'd stop in at Barry's for a trim."

"I'm not sure, either, but I think I heard he'd moved to Florida or somewhere down South."

"It's hard to keep up with all the kids who move away from town. It's bad enough keeping up with the ones who're still here!"

Gracie agreed, thinking at the same time what a joy it was to share with her neighbors and choir friends the delightful goings-on of her only son Arlen and his family, even if they were hundreds of miles away.

When the phone rang the next day, her mind was on a catering job and she was startled to hear Abe Wasserman's voice asking, "Are you by any chance coming my way later on this afternoon, Gracie?"

"I . . . could," she replied. "Of course I'll be there if you need me for something. What's up?"

"Well . . ." His pause seemed long. "I've heard some things recently that I feel certain you'd want to know about."

She blinked. "Things about *me*?"

"Not directly—but if you'd come by after three, when it's usually quiet, I think we can sit down together and I'll share my information with you. Then we can make a plan. . . ."

She glanced at the wall clock, aware that the minutes would weigh heavily until she'd heard the details of what was worrying him. "No problem, Abe dear. I'll be there."

What's this all about? She immediately began to see if she

5

could figure it out. *Lord, can You give me any clues? What's going on? Why does Abe feel the need all of a sudden to talk with me? I wish it didn't sound so ominous.*

But there was lunch to be fixed first and several more calls to be answered. There was also a prayer request, to which she and Uncle Miltie responded together before she passed it on to her best friend and next-door neighbor, Marge Lawrence, whose name followed theirs on their church's list.

Her uncle was snoozing on the couch when Gracie left, so she scrawled a note and placed it on the table, saying she'd be back soon. Gooseberry seemed eager to follow her, but she shoo'd him back inside. "Go keep Uncle Miltie company! Isn't it in your job description to sleep at least twenty hours a day? Do you want me to have to fire you?"

At the deli, Abe didn't bother to ask what she might like to eat or drink. Instead, he finished whipping up a thick chocolate milkshake which he set in front of her on the counter. Bringing his own glass of seltzer with him, he took the stool next to hers. "Thanks for coming."

"I have to say it sounded almost like a command performance."

"Gracie, my good friend, I would never, ever, try commanding you." His lips twitched slightly. "As if it would work, even if I tried!"

"You never know!" She laughed. "Being independent-minded isn't the same as being stubborn. I'll leave that to Estelle or Cordelia, who are far better at it than I!"

Abe chuckled, knowing that Estelle Livett and Cordelia Fountain were two of Willow Bend's doughtiest divas.

His mirth was brief, however and he glanced at her, his brow furrowed. "I've heard stuff these last few days, Gracie, that I suspect you haven't. They're all rumors, I'm sure, yet I feel you should be made aware of them."

She clasped her hands together on the counter, and Abe knew she was taking a moment for needful prayer. Aloud, she said nothing and he continued, "There are stories—not nice ones—going around town."

"About *me*?"

He shook his head. Again he looked sad. "Well, no—at least not directly."

"Then . . . ?"

"They're about Elmo." He shut his eyes for a second.

"That's ridiculous!" A mental image of her adored husband, with his eyes crinkling at the corners as he smiled at her, took her away momentarily.

"Yes, it is," Abe agreed.

"So, out with it! Better to say these thing aloud and keep them out of the shadows where they grow in toxicity, as Elmo used to say."

Abe shifted on his seat, obviously uncomfortable about what

he was about to share. He glanced toward the door, hoping the current lull in business wasn't about to be broken. God must be watching out for them, Gracie thought, since no one had interrupted them so far, not even for a take-out coffee.

She laid her hand on his, which was gripping the edge of the counter. "It's okay, Abe, just tell me what you've heard. Maybe together we can make some sense of it."

His hand clasped hers firmly. "As you know, I try to avoid or ignore as much gossip as possible. So I wasn't the first to be told that somehow evidence has turned up indicating that when he served as mayor, Elmo may have bent the law, been . . . unethical, even."

She stared at him. "What?"

He nodded grimly. "That was my reaction, too. Total disbelief. But since I was overhearing customers' conversations—and feeling guilty about it—I didn't know how to follow up without being a conspicuous busybody."

"I understand, but how much have you been able to piece together?"

"Not enough, that's for sure. It's as though—well, it's strange. What it seems to me is that someone's sowing mere hints or partial clues. Perhaps they're actually trying just to whet curiosity, rather than satisfy it."

"But why? That is strange. What's it mean?" Her mind was racing.

Abe, sensing her anguish, patted her hand. He frowned as he tried to explain, "I gather there are some documents indicating that Elmo may have made deals that weren't quite . . . kosher." He made a face. "And I'm not trying to be funny."

"I know you aren't, Abe dear. It's just all a bit overwhelming. And ridiculous! But rumors are weeds with nasty roots, and I know pulling them out cleanly is never easy. I am so grateful for your alerting me to this problem, and I've never been more proud of Elmo Parks than I am at this moment. His immense and loving spirit did not die in that car accident—it lives on in me and in friends like you."

He nodded. "You're right, Gracie. We're his legacy, and these ugly untruths are like a guerrilla army, hiding from direct sight. Elmo stood for the decency, honesty and love of his community."

She drew in a deep breath and then let it out slowly. "Thank you."

They sat silently for a few moments before she spoke again. "Did you get any idea what he's actually being accused of?"

"No, that's part of the problem. I got the general idea, but no specifics."

"Elmo stopped being mayor when he felt it was time for someone new to serve. Otherwise, he'd have been reelected in a landslide each time—or am I just hopelessly prejudiced?"

Gracie looked at Abe, and he shook his head. "No. People always followed where he led, not because they had to but because they wanted to."

"That's the man I knew," she affirmed. "No matter whether he was mayor or not, he was just plain Elmo Parks, who had no love of titles or honors. Love of God, his family and his town was enough for him."

It was at this moment two women came in. The older one, Alta Fitzpatrick, asked for a piece of cheesecake. "What are the toppings today?" she wanted to know, and then selected cherry for herself and a slice of pound cake for her younger companion.

Gracie slid off her stool to greet them, politely inquiring about Alta's Aunt Augusta Lawson, who'd been in the hospital recently. Alta then asked Gracie to sit with them. "With your regular prayer-walking, Gracie, *you* can get away with all those yummy calories!"

Gracie laughed. She decided not to point out that cherry cheesecake hardly counted as diet fare.

Robin Fitzpatrick, Alta's daughter-in-law, broke in, "I hear you may be running for mayor, Gracie."

Gracie smiled. "What's true is that several people have suggested it. But I haven't agreed."

The women glanced at one another before Robin went on, "I understood that a second delegation was coming to see you about it. They're serious."

"Well, I feel like I barely have enough hours in the day to get done all the things I'm already committed to. To do a really good job of being mayor means being on the job pretty much all the time!"

"But . . ."

Gracie didn't make a practice of interrupting, but she considered this a good time for making an exception. "Elmo, too, I confess, was always busy with other things—but he carried it all off with the ease with which he did everything. Or he made it look easy, even when there were difficult and complex matters facing him."

"Well, Gracie, you have helped get more women elected to the council!" Alta herself was now a town councilwoman.

Gracie smiled. "It did seem to me that, since we make up roughly half the population, we should at least have better representation on the council."

"What inspired me," Alta reminded her, "was your telling us that time about your grandmother who grew up on a farm—in western Pennsylvania, wasn't it? You said that her father's hired man couldn't even read and write, yet he got to go with her dad to vote in every election while *she*, a teacher in their nearby one-room country school, wasn't allowed to vote 'cause she was a woman!"

Gracie nodded. "How she rejoiced once the Nineteenth Amendment was finally ratified! And I heard it so many times that I can still quote it: 'The right of citizens of the United

States to vote shall not be denied or abridged by the United States or by any State on account of sex.'"

Her friend nodded, "So I did a lot of thinking and a lot of praying about running for the council spot, and talked with you and Elmo and others."

"And the rest is history!" Robin quipped. She gave a look of loving pride at her husband's mother with whom she got along so well. "We see before us our most reelected member!"

Alta gazed at Gracie affectionately. "So, Gracie, are you prepared for the kind of lecture you and your husband once gave me?"

Gracie took the last sip of her shake and got to her feet. "Thanks for the vote of confidence, but I'm making no commitment as of now."

"Will you at least think about it?"

"I—suppose I can't avoid doing that, but at this point I just don't feel called to be mayor."

Abe stood by the table, having heard at least the last part of their conversation. "Just so you don't feel 'called' *not* to do it— that's what we're hoping for." He grinned at the Fitzpatricks.

Gracie shook her head in mock exasperation. "You guys never know when to give up, do you?"

She was serious again as she went out the door of the deli, waving at her friends. What Abe had told her couldn't be forgotten, even if the banter with Alta had been a reassuring moment of normalcy.

Hmmm, she reminded herself, it's not exactly normal when your fellow citizens are trying to talk you into running for office!

If ever there was a right moment to drop in on her friend, Rocky Gravino, the proprietor of the *Mason County Gazette*, this was it. As she approached his office, she saw through the expanse of glass that he was busily working at his computer.

He must have sensed her approach, for he glanced around, a welcoming smile appearing instantly, even as his fingers completed whatever thought they'd been in process of transcribing.

She looked at him questioningly. "I picked a bad time?"

He scooped a pile of papers off the chair in front of his desk. "You can't come at a bad time, Gracie, and you know it. Your very presence makes things better."

She could see on his desk that he'd been going over some print-outs. "An editor's work is never done," she told him, "so I thank you for welcoming me as a distraction."

He snorted. "If you read the last Letters to the Editor section, you're aware that some of our readers wish this particular editor would be done with it—for once and for all!"

His chair rolled back a little as he sank down into his seat. Gracie smiled and held out a brown bag into which Abe had placed two toasted and buttered bagels.

"You're a lifesaver, Gracie," Rocky told her. "I had an interview with Tom Ritter this morning and came back to write that up—then got busy. Up 'til now, coffee's been the only thing keeping me going."

"Must I wait to read my copy of the *Gazette* to learn whether you got any mayoral quotes that will impress or amaze Willow Bend?"

He snorted. "I'm working to make them at least a little more interesting than they sounded to me."

He reached for the second bagel. "You know I strive to be editorially unbiased—most of the time. That doesn't alter the fact, however, that I'd been hoping Tom would say he wasn't going to run again this fall."

"Hey, Sherry would have his head on a platter if she had to give up her position as mayor's wife!"

"If she only knew. . . ," Rocky sighed. Her airs and ambitions were often the cause of loud sighs around town, but Sherry Ritter seemed oblivious.

"Why won't you think about running against him? I'd love to cover *your* town hall!"

She laughed. "I'd rather draft you as my press secretary and image consultant."

"Well, the only other alternatives are Harvey and Tony—and either one would be almost as bad as Tom, though in different ways."

"You haven't interviewed them yet?"

Rocky let loose another huge sigh. "Something's wrong,

Gracie. Supposedly both of them are running, but I've got only word-of-mouth confirmation, nothing official."

She nodded. "Knowing them, wouldn't you think they'd be at one another's throats if each was trying for the job again? Yet I saw them at Abe's having breakfast together yesterday, looking decidedly cozy."

"*Hmmph!*" He took a gulp of coffee. "Did they say anything?"

"Very little. They acknowledged my presence, but that was about it."

He sat there studying her until she asked, "What's up?"

"Anyone else acting strange? Different?"

She couldn't resist asking, "In addition to present company?"

He snorted. "I guess I asked for that, didn't I?"

"It does seem that way."

His square hand moved upward, fingers running back through his salt-and-pepper hair. "Look, Gracie, something's coming out of thin air and making your late and much-loved husband its target. Three different people in the last thirty-six hours have whispered about some kind of hanky-panky that supposedly took place while Elmo was mayor."

Gracie cautioned herself to remain calm. "I know. Abe just told me he's heard it, too."

His chair squeaked slightly as he leaned forward. "It's

crazy. The first person I heard it from even advised me to conduct an investigation or something—though he claimed to have no idea what it's all about. Does that make any sense?"

"And the second person? And the third?"

He cocked his head at her. "Seems they all heard roughly the same story, yet nobody has any straight details. It's like mist: You see it and yet you can't touch it. But it's still liable to blindside you!"

"In that case," she began, getting to her feet, "I'm going to stay upbeat. Elmo's reputation needs no defending—after all, anyone can start rumors."

He stood up also. "Okay, Gracie, my girl, I respect that good attitude of yours. But I know you're even more concerned than I am. Just remember, however, that you've got many devoted friends. Including me. And we were all Elmo's friends, too."

"I appreciate that."

"And I'll be keeping an ear to the ground."

"You'll let me know if you find out anything more?"

"Of course."

"Then we'll clear that mist away as soon as it starts blowing in our direction again. If gossip and rumor are the fallout of bad faith, then we'll just combat it with good!"

"Amen, Gracie," Rocky said solemnly.

GRACIE HAD REFRAINED from telling Uncle Miltie or Marge anything about the Elmo rumors. However, later that afternoon, Gracie's uncle came stomping into the kitchen. "You're not going to believe this."

She looked at him fondly. "Try me."

What he told her had the same shape, but no more substance, than what she'd already heard. "Thank God my friends don't fall for this baloney! But there are probably some people who might, those who never knew Elmo."

On their way to choir practice that evening, Marge contributed a story about someone at her gift shop that afternoon mentioning suspicions concerning the late Elmo Parks. It turned out that the entire choir of Eternal Hope Church also had heard the rumors.

Gracie wondered who hadn't!

Barb Jennings, the choir director, finally called her distracted flock back to order by banging her baton against the metal music stand. "We are here to practice singing praises to the Lord! We will now get back to doing our Father's business by once more running through our anthem for this Sunday, 'The Earth Is the Lord's.'"

There was a continuing murmur until the brief two-bar introduction was over and the first words were sung. "No, *no*, NO!" Barb cried, again banging the hapless stand. "This is a song of rejoicing, not a dirge! Now let's start again from the beginning!"

This time they came in together, and Gracie found she could temporarily set aside the tension gripping her heart. She especially savored hearing the parts in the chorus when soloists called out various items for which they were thankful.

You've done it again, God, haven't You? We've practiced this for the last several weeks, and I've soloed that same part near the end each time. Yet now, troubled and unhappy, I heard myself singing out those words that I needed above all else to remember, "For all people on the earth who are trying to do right"—with my friends affirming, "We sincerely sing Your praise."

As Barb closed her music folder, Lester Twomley said, "I just thought of a way that might help us figure where these rumors about Elmo started. Let's go to one of the kids' classrooms, and put on the blackboard the names of those who told each of us about it."

Although hoping for useful results, Gracie had to admit, after a good ten minutes of writing name after name, that there still seemed no pattern. "This doesn't seem to be getting us anywhere, does it? But, thanks anyway, all of you, especially Les," smiling at him as she got up from the child-sized chair.

"It was an excellent idea and I've copied what's on the board, so let's erase it before we leave. Maybe, as time goes by and we continue to pay attention to who's saying what, it will all begin to make more sense!"

Another day passed. In the post office, several people seemed especially caring or encouraging. One friend, Cordelia Fountain, even put an arm around her and said, "Keep your chin up, Gracie. We're praying for you and your Uncle George."

The tourist home owner was one of the few Willow Benders who sometimes called Uncle Miltie by his given name instead of his nickname. Gracie couldn't help but feel touched, since Cordelia's usual manner was more reserved.

Her uncle said when told of Cordelia's comment, "The only thing I can think of to explain this mass insanity is that someone's trying to get at you, so you won't want to be elected. Get at you indirectly, I mean."

Gracie shook her head impatiently. "That doesn't make sense. I'm not running for anything!"

"Then," he put in with a crooked grin, "maybe it's a case of reverse psychology. Now you just might end up doing it out of sheer stubbornness!"

"You've got to be kidding!"

He laughed. "Stranger things have happened."

"Well, if you believe that, I'd better have Cordelia pray for you even harder!"

The rest of Friday was spent in the kitchen. Many of her church's women members had decided to have a soup-and-bake sale the following day, and Gracie was the backbone of such endeavors. "You know," she told her uncle, "there are more logical ways of making money for our mission project.

"When you come right down to it, Uncle Miltie, if each woman gave only twice as much cash as she's spending on ingredients—to compensate in small part for the time and effort she'd otherwise be expending—we'd probably end up with as much as we'll earn this way."

"But you're overlooking the vanity factor," he reminded her. "Mabel Loomis loves the raves for her chili con carne and Eleanor for her berry-custard pies."

She had to agree: Logic didn't apply to every situation. "You're right, of course. And it's about tradition, too. Some of our older members remember those times in their lives when many were unable to give much money, and the bounty of their farms and gardens made up for it. Deliciously!"

She took the large metal sheet from the oven and transferred the cookies to wire racks. "At least that's the last of these. And I'll be getting up very early in the morning to make the cinnamon buns."

"You'll leave a pan of those here for us to eat, won't you?"

"I promise."

He licked his lips in anticipation. "I know there are never any of your cinnamon buns left over. They're usually gone before you have both feet inside the church kitchen!"

"I'd at least planned to leave you some chocolate chip cookies. I can't have you starving to death."

"I'm a nut for chocolate chips!" he quipped. "Walnut, peanut or pecan!"

"Well, these are plain," she told him.

"Then I'm just plain nutty."

Gracie groaned softly.

The sky was not yet showing signs of morning when Gracie went down to the kitchen to start the dry yeast multiplying rapidly in sugar-saturated warm water. In less than an hour she was able to punch down the raised dough and started forming the first third of it into an elongated rectangle that she then spread with butter and sprinkled liberally with sugar and cinnamon.

Starting from the long side, she rolled it over and over, finally laying the thick rope-like dough seam-down at the back of the counter and repeating the process with the other thirds.

She'd done this so many times she didn't have to measure as she melted butter in a saucepan, dumped in brown sugar, molasses, some cinnamon, and added a little corn syrup. As soon as the stirred mixture came to a boil, she began spooning some of it to cover the bottom of the baking pans she'd set out.

She'd let the oven warm slightly while cutting the first "rope" into inch-wide slices which she now placed flat-side-down in the prepared pan. These portions now had the opportunity to rise slowly in the lukewarm oven as she repeated the process again and again with all three portions. Then, keeping her promise to her uncle, she placed all of the "ends" into one last cake pan.

By the time Uncle Miltie appeared to say good morning, the first pans were already baking. He came, already dressed for his day of helping with the bake sale, to look through the glass-fronted oven. "They look as good as they smell, Gracie! But then, they always do!"

"Thanks. Those on the top shelf will be coming out in a few minutes, then I'll move those on the lower one to the top and put in the next pans."

"Anything I can do to help?"

"I think it's all okay—you just keep your appetite and your appreciation ready!"

"It won't be hard!"

"Actually," Gracie said, glancing around, "you could put those cookies over there onto the trays. After that, we'll wrap them for traveling."

"We make a pretty good team," he told her.

She smiled. "You hadn't noticed before?"

"You bet I have!" he assured her. "Why else would this old coot who came for a visit all those years ago have decided never to leave?"

"Maybe because I wanted you to stay even more than you wanted to."

"Now that I maybe should argue, but let's just say I'm eternally grateful that our arrangement's worked out so well!"

"Amen!" Gracie said. Both of them, she saw, were unashamed of the tears that had come into the corners of their eyes. "Here's a tissue," she said to him. And he took it, with a loving look at her.

"Is it all right if I do some bake sale spending now, Gracie, instead of going to the church?" Betsy Griswold had stuck her head in at the kitchen door.

Uncle Miltie got his response out first. He told their neighbor, "Your money for missions is just as valuable here as there."

"Great! I've got a houseful of kids this weekend, and the little darlings love Gracie's sticky buns even more than John and I do! Plus, with their energy, they burn the calories just by looking at them!" She laid some money on the counter as she began selecting her purchase.

"That's too much money," Uncle Miltie told her, starting to get out his wallet.

Betsy shook her head. "It's not too much for Gracie's baking, that's for sure. And if it's more than you'd actually be charging, that's okay, too. It's for a good cause."

Realizing her uncle was about to insist on giving back some of the money, Gracie put in smoothly, "That's generous of you, and we do appreciate it very much. Every cent we take in will be sent directly to our mission work in Honduras."

She lifted the still-warm rolls into the shopping bag their neighbor had brought with her. "Oh, and I'll take a tray of cookies, too," Betsy added. "They'll keep if they don't get eaten . . . even if there's little chance of that."

Gracie drove across the parking lot and was pulling up to the door of Eternal Hope's Family Activity Center before she saw Rocky's car being maneuvered into a spot nearby. Clambering out of the driver's seat, he called to her crossly, "I've been waiting for you! Who'd ever think I'd be early and you late?"

Gracie laughed, but Uncle Miltie jumped to her defense. "Well, if you'd gotten up at five-thirty and worked steadily from then till now, you'd understand the baker's side of things!"

Rocky couldn't hide his grin. "Well, I wanted first crack at what you're bringing. What is it this time?"

"Cinnamon rolls and cookies," she told him. "And I intend

to help out with the soup pots now. You know I have an advanced degree in vigorous stirring."

"Well, that sounds more like my line, but before you take up your spoon, let me have a dozen cookies and," looking at what Uncle Miltie was removing from the back seat, "some of those buns."

Thus Gracie got to hand to Eleanor McIver, who was in charge of the cash box, their first thirty dollars of the day. And before the sale had even officially begun. *Dear Lord*, Gracie prayed, *don't consider me too prideful if I take pleasure in the satisfaction others take in my cooking skills. And I know I jumped the gun, but it was for a good cause. I couldn't disappoint Rocky, especially not if he actually showed up early!*

Soon the church activity center was humming. The nourishing soups made by the Turner twins, Tish and Tyne, and some of the other choir members were a hit: chilled gazpacho, chicken corn, cheddar cheese, beef-vegetable, and split pea with ham. "*Mmm, mmm* good," said Uncle Miltie, sniffing the air.

Soon, however, he complained that he had little to do, so Gracie suggested, "How about acting as official greeter? Keep the hellos coming and the jokes at a minimum, and point the way to all the deliciousness on display here, using as many synonyms for mouth-watering as you can possibly come up with."

"I can do that," he happily agreed. "But there may be a way to make money off my jokes—what do you think of my charging for every one I don't tell?"

Gracie laughed. Her uncle wore a thoughtful expression as he headed out of the kitchen.

"Good luck!" she called after him. Then she became absorbed in making sure that fresh supplies of the home-cooked bounty remained at the ready. She hummed happily as she worked.

Uncle Miltie didn't return to the kitchen for nearly an hour, and then it was to say, "I've made forty bucks keeping my jokes to myself."

Gracie, who was about to take a break herself for a bowl of the split pea soup and some of Rick Harding's homemade bread, looked at him incredulously. "That's amazing!" she said. "Wait 'til Marge hears this!"

"Maybe," he admitted, "they wanted to contribute but weren't so hungry. Or else maybe they were so hungry they didn't want to waste time on the way to the food."

"Whoever they were, they know you, that's for sure!"

He made a mock bow. "George Morgan, fundraiser extra-ordinaire at your service!"

"You know, Eleanor says we've already brought in more money than we did last year," Gracie added.

"Splendid!" crowed Uncle Miltie. "There's still some soup left. What will you do with it?"

"After we leave here, some of us will deliver whatever's left to those folks who couldn't get here, and to the shut-ins."

"Can I come with you?"

"Only if you don't charge me!"

About forty minutes later they loaded up Fannie Mae, Gracie's trusty old blue Cadillac. At the homes of several pinochle buddies and other friends from the senior center, Uncle Miltie slowly and carefully made his way in with the filled containers.

But Gracie wanted to make the delivery herself at Hattie Bomboy's. She got out and first tried the heavy knocker on the huge old house's massive front door before ringing the bell. Eventually the door opened just a crack, then a bit farther.

The small, somewhat bent woman welcomed her with pleasure. "Gracie! I'm so pleased to see you." The door squeaked in protest as it was opened fully. "Come in, come in!"

Gracie stepped inside the dark foyer, which seemed nearly as big as her own living room. "We just finished having a soup-and-baked-goods sale," she said. "We sold a lot, but I thought perhaps you'd enjoy a quart of the soup that was left."

"That sounds wonderful." Hattie started to turn. "Wait right here while I get my purse."

Gracie put her hand out, touching Hattie's slender shoulder with careful respect. "Hattie, dear, this was extra, and I bring it to you as a gift. Really, that's how I want it, and the sale already was a huge success!"

Gracie could see the uncertainty of her friend and understood that it was embarrassment and pride that made Hattie, whose family used to be among the wealthiest of Willow

Bend, hesitate about accepting anything that might smack of charity. "Honestly, we sold more than ever before, Hattie, and now we'd like to share the rest."

Gracie could only guess what was in Hattie's mind, but her hostess's pale blue eyes looked up into hers as she reached for the jar. "Thanks, then. I know it's delicious and I look forward to it."

Learning that there were more deliveries to be made, Hattie asked, "Are you by any chance taking some to my brother?"

Gracie hadn't planned to but, hey, why can't she change her itinerary? "Uncle Miltie and I are, in fact, going to Miles's next. Would you like to ride along?"

The wrinkled face broke into a shy smile. "I wouldn't want to inconvenience you."

"It's a lovely idea," Gracie assured her. "We're going right there, and have plenty of room in the car for you."

"But..."

"We won't be able to stay long, but it's a chance for a visit and then we'll drop you off back here."

Hattie thought for a moment before saying, "I will come with you."

"Great!"

Hattie glanced down at the jar in her hand. "I'd better put this in the refrigerator right away, then I'll be ready."

"Take your time," Gracie said warmly. "I'm just glad you thought to ask me." *Lord, please forgive me my little white lie, for the sake of this brother and sister . . . well, actually half-brother and sister.*

Uncle Miltie had lived with Gracie long enough to not be surprised when she returned to the car with the elderly woman in tow, explaining, "Hattie's riding along with us to take some of the vegetable soup to Miles. We can then drop her off back here on our way to the Johnsons."

"Hello, Hattie," he greeted her. "Haven't seen much of you lately. How have you been feeling?"

"*Hmm.* Some arthritis and not as much energy as I'd like— but other than that, I'm pretty good."

"Glad to hear it." He was looking around the grounds, undoubtedly noting how little was being done with the perennials in various beds, though the grass was mowed. "Do you have a boy or someone to take care of the yard? A neighbor?"

She shook her head. "I used to, but it's awfully hard any more to get anyone who really wants to work. It used to be that high school boys liked to make money of their own, but it seems those days are gone—that parents just give them whatever they want."

"So who mows the yard?"

"I do, of course—at least most of the time—though some-times I have no choice but to get somebody from one of those lawncare companies to help out. That's what Miles does now—in fact, I believe he has them come on a regular basis."

Gracie let the other two do most of the talking as she drove across town. There'd been a time when Hattie and her brother hadn't gotten along very well at all, so it was good to learn they now talked on the phone every day or two.

But it was still startling to have seen Hattie eager to come along while free food was being delivered to her eccentric and stubborn half-brother. Gracie never would have thought of it on her own since, in her mind, Miles Stevens could have bought everything that had been on sale earlier at the church: soup, buns and the furnishings, too.

MILES STEVENS, coming to the door of his own large house, looked nothing like the wealthy, retired banker he was. His thinning hair stuck straight up, and he was wearing a threadbare gray cardigan over a wrinkled white cotton shirt unbuttoned at the top.

On his feet were black dress shoes, only one of which was polished to a high gloss.

He glanced from Gracie to his sister, who immediately explained about the soup left over from the church mission fundraiser. He seemed at first almost to recoil from the jar held out to him, but then, as Hattie had done, he offered to pay for it.

Hattie literally thrust it into his hand. "Of course you'll accept it, Miles," she stated firmly. "Gracie brought me some, too. The cooks could have just taken it home to eat or have frozen it for later, but they chose to give it to some of us who couldn't get to Eternal Hope today. It would be terribly rude to refuse it!"

His hand slowly closed around it. "Thank you, Gracie—and you, too, Hattie." The words themselves were quite formal, but then he allowed his strained smile to relax into one seemingly much more genuine. "I haven't eaten good homemade vegetable soup for ages."

I wonder what you do eat, Gracie thought to herself. *There's been no woman living in this house since your mother died, and that's got to be at least twenty-five years. Do you bother cooking for yourself?* Her actual words, however, were, "We're pretty habitual soup-makers, the Eternal Hope choir. Perhaps you could come and eat a big bowl with the rest of us next time."

"Perhaps." He shrugged. "But I don't much enjoy eating out."

"Me, neither," Hattie stated. "And if you cook soup, you end up with so much you're eating it for a week!"

It was on the tip of Gracie's tongue to mention that if Hattie did cook some, she could share it with her brother. *It's truly none of my business, Lord, I understand that.*

"Maybe the next time you could freeze some of it," Gracie suggested instead. "That's what I do for Uncle Miltie and myself."

Hattie nodded. "I could—but it's simpler just to eat what

comes from my meals-on-wheels. And Miles occasionally takes me with him to the grocery store, so I stock up on all kinds of things then . . ."

Her half-brother didn't respond to that, so Gracie broke in, "Look, Hattie, Uncle Miltie and I still have a few stops to make. How about you staying here and visiting for perhaps a half hour while we finish? We can come back and get you and you can go with us while we do some grocery shopping for ourselves."

Lord, I hope I didn't jump into that too quickly. Miles looks more put out than relieved by the prospect of Hattie's staying a while. But I'm sure I've done the right thing.

Hattie, when they got to the Willow Mart, at first seemed not to need much. It didn't occur to Gracie that her friend had little money with her, but Uncle Miltie understood. "Might as well do some serious shopping while we're here, that way we can help carry in your bags," he said, handing her some bills from his wallet.

She looked unhappy, but listened to him as he went on, "Myself, I don't much enjoy shopping, so I always carry extra money. That way I can do lots of it while I'm at it—can get it over with." He smiled encouragingly at her.

She nodded and put out a hand to accept the offered notes. "Well, you can be sure I'll write you a check as soon as we get home."

They returned to the fresh fruit and vegetable section so she could buy a few more potatoes, bananas, and three apples. She exchanged a half-dozen eggs for a dozen and chose a name brand cereal she especially liked instead of the cheaper one.

In the end, Hattie wound up with two more bags than Gracie, greatly to the satisfaction of the latter.

As Uncle Miltie fastened his seatbelt after helping carry in Hattie's groceries, he noted, "That's the first time I've ever been inside."

"What did you think?"

It wasn't until the car started to move that he replied, "Sort of a mausoleum, isn't it?"

"I—hadn't thought of it that way, but yes, it is. I doubt she's done any updating or decorating since her parents died, long before I knew her. At least, it doesn't look like it."

"Sad, isn't it?"

She nodded. "I don't know how well-off she is, but one or two pieces of furniture, like that lovely old desk, would probably keep her in food and heat for a year—maybe the rest of her life."

Gracie sighed. "The thing is, however, that it's *home*. I'm sure she doesn't notice that everything's so outdated and inconvenient, and shabby, to boot. And just because something might be valuable, there's no reason for her to sell it."

"Of course not," he agreed.

❧

34

It's Sunday already. I know every day is Yours, dear Lord, but this one especially so. Gracie got out of bed and headed for the shower, finding herself singing snatches of that morning's choir anthem.

"The earth is the Lord's and the fullness thereof,
We will rejoice and be glad.
The earth is the Lord's, and the people therein,
We will rejoice and be glad.
It's easy to be down, it's easy to be blue—
What we should be doing is bring our trials to You,
You, Lord, are powerful, You are always true.
We will rejoice and be glad.
The earth is the Lord's and the fullness thereof,
We will rejoice and be glad.
The earth is the Lord's, and the people therein,
We will rejoice and be glad...."

Uncle Miltie looked up from the morning newspaper spread out over much of the kitchen table. "You sure sounded upbeat there in the shower this morning!"

She laughed. "There's nothing like a shower to convince you you're ready for the Metropolitan Opera!"

He grinned. "*Hmmm,* It's a shame most church music doesn't give altos a chance to do more than harmonize."

She walked over to check the teakettle. A light ribbon of steam was rising from the spout.

"Is there still a cinnamon roll for me?" she asked, seeing one on his plate.

"Only if I go into my secret stash," he confessed. "But I will."

"Thank you," she said dryly. "Next time I guess I'll have to make my own hidden stockpile."

"No," Uncle Miltie said, "no matter how greedy I sound, I'll always share, I promise."

Gracie looked over her Sunday school lesson for the next half hour until he came into the house with a mass of chrysanthemums. She hurriedly got out two large vases in which to arrange them, and they were soon on their way to church, with Uncle Miltie carefully balancing them against sudden turns and unexpected braking.

As soon as she parked, Gracie reached over to hold the flowers for him as he got out of the car. Their good friend Joe Searfoss, four spaces away, called out to ask if they could use help.

Gracie let the men take care of placing the vases in the sanctuary. As she proceeded in later with the choir, she had to smile. She hadn't expected to see the vases left sitting on the floor on either side of the pulpit. If she'd carried them in, they'd be sitting up on the carved wooden stands meant for exactly that purpose.

The children's sermon began with Pastor Paul speaking about untruths. He asked the youngsters in the congregation to think about any recent fibs they might have indulged in.

There was some obvious squirming, but only a few worried-looking kids nodded or spoke up. One boy with an unruly cowlick qualified his fib, "But it was not a *bad* lie—and I'm not gonna say what it was."

Paul smiled at him. "To be perfectly honest, Johnny, I'm afraid we've all sometimes said things that aren't completely true. Even me."

"*You?*" He looked horrified at the thought of his pastor's lying.

"There are so many different ways of not telling the truth," Pastor Paul replied, looking from Johnny Lewis to congregants in the pews all around him. "There are actual lies we tell to get out of trouble—or to cover up things we've done that we don't want others to know about. And there are things we say that are only half-true, like that we're 'too busy' to be of help to others.

"And we sometimes pass on stories about other people even if we don't know if they're true or not. Sometimes those can be the very worst kinds of things to say, because these stories can grow and grow and grow. Each person who hears them passes them on, sometimes even adding their own version or opinion about what's been told to them.

"I'd like us to try something here. I'm going to whisper something to you, Jill," he said to the little girl at the end, and did so. "Now, I want you to whisper what I told you to Kevin, who will pass it on to Pete—and it will go right down the line, okay?"

As the last youngster received the words, Paul asked, "Caitlin, would you please tell me and the congregation what you heard?"

"*Hmmm*, you said you'd gone out yesterday and watched a ball game and someone got hurt and you cried."

"Thank you," he said. "And now, Jill, would you tell us what you understood me to say?"

The girl giggled. "It wasn't that."

"What was it then?"

"You said you went to the park, and you climbed up in the bleachers behind where the batter and catcher stand. It got dark and the wind was making loud noises and so you went home."

"Thank you, Jill, that's pretty much what I did say." He looked down the line of children, some insisting that was *not* what was told to them. Paul then explained to them—and to the whole congregation—how easy it is to not pass things on carefully, and how common it is for any person receiving a message to have a different interpretation of what was said.

"Not one person here had any reason or intention not to keep my simple little story straight, yet even the place and what or who was crying got changed.

"There are always stories going around. Everywhere in the world. And Willow Bend hears its share. Please, kids," he cautioned them, looking over their heads at the pews behind them, "and, you older folks, as well, try not to believe all that you hear. And even things you see are not necessarily what they seem to be.

"Gossip seems like fun much of the time, especially when a good friend shares it. But it is never, ever fun to the person—or people—it's about. And that's what we must remember, especially since, often, it's untrue in the first place."

Paul added a few more things, including what Jesus would have His children do and say, before releasing the children to go to Junior Church. His glance never turned toward Gracie, but she was sure that Paul's chosen theme was a result of the seemingly reckless rumors concerning her beloved Elmo.

The anthem went well, and as the choir members called out, identifying those things that made them especially thankful, Gracie felt a burst of love for her church community and her Lord. She was always grateful for her own blessings, and her spirit seemed to soar in happy affirmation. Oh, that the Willow Benders seated before her would truly hear what Paul was telling them!

He now surprised her.

"Barb, may I ask a favor of you and the choir? Would you please play that last part again, with the choir singing only the 'We will rejoice and be glad' part? I'd like to give individuals in our congregation the opportunity of calling out things for which they are grateful."

As Barb started playing, he explained, "I'll start it off, so you get the idea. Then please feel free to join in."

"For all these wonderful people who are so conscientious and faithful!" he declared in a strong voice. The congregation followed suit: "For my mother's love and my mother-in-law's too!" "For the bounty of our farms and the dedication of our farmers!" "For the young people who are our future!" "For my husband whose wisdom I cherish!"

Gracie felt moisture collecting in her eyes, especially at this last, but she was smiling as she sang the choral response, "We will rejoice and be glad...."

Her son called from New York City that afternoon. "Hi, Mom, how are things going in Willow Bend on this beautiful day?"

"Arlen, I'm so happy to hear your voice! We're doing great here. How are things in the big city?"

"Just fine, at least everything we're involved with." He brought her up-to-date on their most recent activities, including the fact that Wendy was helping the teacher in their son's first-grade class prepare for the school's Fall Fling. "I doubt that they have any idea what a pro they have in our Elmo's mother. There's some sort of a dance they're going to perform, and she's already got it all sketched out. They may very well go into shock when she shows it to them tomorrow."

"Well, it's wonderful that she can contribute, making use of her abilities as a dancer and dance teacher. She's a remarkable young woman."

40

"She is, isn't she?" His voice was filled with pride.

"It's been lovely to see her recitals on a couple of my visits. I was impressed by what she got out of even the youngest of her students!"

"That's the time to get them started—at least that's what she tells me." He laughed. "It's a miracle she even *looked* at your son, Mom, since I somehow seem to have been born with three left feet!"

"Well, even if you trip over all of them continually, I'm as proud of you as I am of Wendy, and I wish your dad were here to share that pride with me."

Inadvertently, Gracie let out a long sigh.

"Mom?" Arlen's voice tightened. "What's wrong?"

She gave a slightly embarrassed laugh. "Nothing."

There was silence at the other end. Finally, she asked, "Are you still there?"

"Yeah, but I know you're in the midst of a big problem and that 'nothing' hardly begins to describe it. I'm just trying to figure out the right questions to ask to get you to talk."

"Don't be silly, dear...."

"Just let me get one thing cleared up first: Are you in any personal danger?"

"Of course not!"

"Are there any recently deceased bodies?"

"Not that I'm aware of. I..."

"Violence to friends or neighbors?"

41

"No!"

"Missing funds or accounts?"

"I—don't think so."

"*Uh-oh*—so that's a possibility." He listened to her sigh again. "Whose money? Yours?"

She laughed, but weakly. "No, Arlen, I haven't done anything with my money, or anyone else's, for that matter."

"Okay, Mom, I'm bracing myself for the worst. What's up?"

Oh, dear Lord, how well he knows me! Here I am, trying to keep my own counsel, and yet he knows I'm fretting about something. I just hate the thought of upsetting him about these stupid rumors. . . .

"Earth to Mom?" he joked.

She took a deep breath. "Well, there is something bothering me, but I simply hoped I'd never have to tell you about it."

"Forget that! I'm your son, remember?"

So she told about the rumors. "It's all so strange, Arlen! There are apparently no specifics, just generalities—only hints about wrongdoing, and probably in the area of malfeasance— but goodness knows if that's even it.

"If it were someone other than dad, we might suspect something of a—moral nature. . . ."

"That's totally out of the question!"

"I know. Your father was an exemplary man, Arlen, he really was." She felt her body tremble with the strain she was facing, and she was glad Arlen was not there to see her. What she longed for were her husband's arms.

"We were truly blessed, weren't we?" Arlen said.

"Yes, we were—we are."

"Agreed! So what are we going to do about this situation?"

"We?" Gracie was startled

"We!" he repeated. "What have you done so far to find out what's going on?"

She thought for a moment. "Not much, personally. Abe and Rocky are trying to find out what's going on, and so are the choir members."

"Have you checked with Herb yet? Might as well get law enforcement in on this, too."

"I doubt it's a legal matter."

"But you aren't sure it's not, are you?"

"You win on that one, dear. Okay, I'll check in with him soon."

" 'Soon,' meaning when?"

She laughed. "Don't be too hard on me, Arlen. This is all horrible, but it's also a shock, and it's still so nebulous!"

"Well, what's not nebulous is me! I'll be calling back tomorrow. And, if necessary, I'll be arriving on your doorstep with my deerstalker hat and magnifying glass. Just call me Sherlock Parks!"

"Dear, if my failure to pin all this down means a visit from you, I'll spend the rest of the day walking with Gooseberry, or cleaning a closet or two. I won't even consider taking up anything more useful!"

"Whatever you do, Mom, just remember I'm going to be checking on you . . . regularly!"

REALLY, GOOSEBERRY!" Gracie had first tried explaining the situation to her cat and then had attempted to ignore him. Now, again, he was at the kitchen door, issuing insistent *meows* intended to lure her outside.

"The rain's pouring down, and I don't feel like getting soaked this early in the morning."

He cocked his head, gave what seemed a sigh of resignation, and lay down right against the door, chin resting on his crossed paws, green eyes staring unblinkingly at her.

She chuckled and, with a slight shake of her head, returned to studying the books and recipe cards spread out before her. John Ball had contacted her a couple of days earlier and asked if she'd cater a special dinner. "I know it's not much warning, but we only just decided on a plan of action. The twins' birthday is soon—and, with no coaxing from them at all, Bill and I came to the mutual conclusion a surprise party would be fun."

"How lovely! But how many people are you planning to invite? And do you have a budget?"

He seemed at a loss. Maybe talking it over with Bill Anderson, his brother-in-law, would be more useful. Meanwhile, she'd work up some suggestions.

Gooseberry's swift march across the kitchen floor was a sure sign that Uncle Miltie was headed downstairs. Gracie smiled as Gooseberry went through his morning routine, lifting his chin up to be scratched on its underside the moment her uncle hove into view.

"Sleep okay?" she asked.

"Yup," he replied. "And you?"

"Fine," she said. "A few restless moments, but talking to Arlen was just what I needed."

Uncle Miltie growled, "I wish I could get my hands on whoever is behind these miserable mumblings around town!"

"Can I get you breakfast?"

"You've already got your hands full, my girl. I can take care of putting bread into the toaster, and there's an excellent array of jams, as you know."

The toaster popped, and he took out the two slices of whole wheat toast, slathering them with apricot preserves. Taking a big bite, he rolled his eyes. "Some might call this toast crumby, but I say it's fit for a king!"

Gracie shook her head in fond exasperation. Then she

watched Gooseberry stretch and hop onto the windowsill.

"I think the storm's nearly over," Uncle Miltie declared.

"*Shhhh,*" she cautioned. "Someone's been trying to get me to take a w-a-l-k with him, and I've been pointing out it's much too wet."

"I'm cat-a-tonic, then, which means I shut up right this minute!" He clamped his lips shut to demonstrate.

Gracie had just finished a third possible menu for the twins' surprise party when the first weak hint of sunshine brightened the windows. "Okay, kiddo, I think we can go out now."

Gooseberry had been near the door before, but now he was impatient to push past it into the great outdoors.

"I'm coming, my friend!" she assured him.

She'd recently bought a new tape of praise hymns, but she left it and her player behind. "After any rain, there's always enough birdsong to keep me musically enthralled by nature's melodies," she told the feline waiting for her.

For his part, music wasn't his thing, and he didn't seem overly impressed by the chirps and trills. But he did enjoy chasing a chipmunk that happened across his path. The little striped creature escaped, however, much to Gracie's relief.

Later that afternoon she was about to work in one of the flowerbeds, but suddenly heard the low beep of a lightly tapped horn. She turned around to see Herb Bower, Willow Bend's police chief, waving as he drove past. Oh, dear, I meant to stop by the station and talk to him!

Well, since he seemed to be heading in the direction of his office, she decided to walk over there now. It was only a few blocks, and she'd promised Arlen she'd talk to Herb about the troubling situation. *As if I had any idea of what's going on,* she said to herself ruefully.

As she walked inside, Lucille Murphy, the daytime dispatcher, glanced up from her computer. "Hi, Gracie, come on in!" She then looked past Gracie. "Where's your funny sidekick?"

Gracie put a finger to her lips. "Don't ever tell Gooseberry that I sneaked out while he was napping."

"Your secret's safe with me." Lucille chuckled before asking, "You here for Herb?"

"I'd like to see him if he's free—he just drove by my place, and I remembered something I wanted to talk over with him."

Lucille stood up and started back the short hallway. "I'm pretty sure he can see you now, but I'll just check first."

Moments later Herb was following the dispatcher out of his office. "Come on back, Gracie," he welcomed her.

She did so, explaining, "I'm here under orders from my son."

"If he wants you to talk to me, then there must be a good reason."

"He thinks so."

"That's enough for me. But, then, I'm always interested in what you have to say. You know that."

"Well, what I did was tell him that I had not discussed something with you which perhaps I should have."

Herb motioned to the chair beside his desk. "I'll bet Marybeth mentioned our upsetting discussion at choir practice," she said, looking squarely at him.

"She did. But since I hadn't heard anything from you, I'd hoped the situation might be less worrisome than she indicated."

Gracie looked down at her hands clasped in her lap before replying. Her voice was low. "It's like fighting smoke when you don't know where the fire is. Elmo Parks has no way of defending himself against these rumors, and I know he would never have comitted the least impropriety. The question is, is it about Elmo . . . or about me, really?"

"Do you know what's actually being said?"

She shook her head. "Nothing specific—only that he's being maligned or that his reputation is. But what am I supposed to do when nobody's willing or able to tell me what's going on?"

"I agree—that does make it difficult. . . ."

She shifted in her chair. "Help me, Herb. I have to know the truth. What's happening?"

She was fairly sure his frown was not directed at her. "I'm puzzled, too, Gracie. The checking I've done so far has led nowhere—maybe back just one or two people, beyond which no one seems to know anything."

"I know he made some of our citizens less than happy when, as mayor, he refused to get people off the hook for parking violations and stuff like that. But would those individuals still be angry about such small potatoes?"

"One wouldn't think so. Of course, as mayor he presided over meetings where unpopular measures were sometimes brought up and acted upon."

She agreed. "But the trouble with that scenario is that, as mayor, he ran the town council meetings but could never vote for or against anything. So how could someone carry a grudge against him all this time?"

He shrugged. "I've no idea."

"Do you think it's at all possible that this effort is being directed at me rather than at Elmo?"

Herb raised an eyebrow. "Go on."

"I'm not sure how to go on. It's just that this seemed to start after a few people came to urge me to run for mayor. That's when I first started hearing about the rumors, anyway.

"What I told them was that I was honored. But I said I had no intention of running for anything. I thought I'd gotten the point across that I dearly love Willow Bend, but I don't wish to be its mayor."

He nodded. "Unfortunately, if you don't choose to run, that leaves just Tony Randolph and Harvey Smith up against Tom. And that, I gather, is unacceptable to many of our voters."

"Meaning that Tom could get reelected?"

"I think he could very well get reelected." Herb looked troubled.

She hadn't thought of how Tom Ritter's reelection might affect Herb. "I forgot—the mayor has authority over the police department, doesn't he?"

"He does indeed."

There was a moment's silence before she murmured, "I never knew just why or on what grounds Elmo got rid of Syd Browning. . . ."

"That was before I came to Willow Bend."

Gracie understood that this was his way of saying he was not going to discuss any of the circumstances surrounding the removal of his predecessor. "Do you know where he is these days?"

"Not exactly."

"He apparently made threats at the time—though Elmo never wanted to share those with me."

"Which was wise."

"Tell me, Herb, is there any chance that it might be Sydney Browning who's orchestrating all this?"

"I doubt it—though anything's possible, I suppose."

There was silence again for a moment before she drew in a deep breath. "You'll never know what a shock it was to find that, once Syd was discharged, it meant that Elmo, as mayor, had to take over as acting chief of police until another was found!"

His grin was a crooked one. "Which is where I came in."

"Thank God!" She looked at him with respect and affection. "I've given thanks for you many times, my friend."

"I appreciate your friendship, as well as your help. Even when it's unexpected."

"Hey, we got you into this!" She could laugh about it now. "The least I can do is help where I'm able."

"I don't know what I'd do without you, Gracie. Or Willow Bend, for that matter."

"Just find out who's starting the rumors—and keeping them going—if you can."

"I've been trying, Gracie," he assured her, "and I intend to continue."

"While you're busy with that, I'll try to think of someone else who can run against Tom, someone who'll have a real chance."

It was a promise to both him and herself.

As she walked back into her kitchen, Uncle Miltie announced, "Tomorrow's the day for Gooseberry to go to the veterinarian for his shots."

"I know."

They both noticed the cat suddenly stalk into the other room. Uncle Miltie shook his head. "Is it possible he understands?"

"Who knows?"

Uncle Miltie chuckled. Who knew what cats were capable of comprehending?

"Actually," Gracie said, "he doesn't seem to mind going to get his shots—not that much, anyway. Davena Wilkins has a great bedside manner!"

"I like her, too," Uncle Miltie admitted. "Gooseberry's not the only one."

"You know. . . ?" The idea she suddenly had was so unexpected that Gracie didn't even finish it.

"What?"

"I was just thinking. . ."

"About what?"

"What would you think of Dave's running for mayor?"

"Would she be willing?"

"I have no idea, but she'd certainly do a great job."

"No doubt about that—if she could only be persuaded."

Gracie did a lot of praying that night—and was pleased in the morning when her uncle confided, "I've been praying that Dave will say yes when you ask her."

Even their joint prayer before breakfast contained that request, although Gracie thoughtfully added, ". . . if it wouldn't be too much for her, Lord, in addition to all her veterinary duties."

At Dr. Wilkins's office, Gooseberry sat beside his mistress on the comfortable waiting room sofa, purring away.

"Hello, Gooseberry," Davena Wilkins greeted him in her warm, pleasant voice as she ran her hand along his back. "You're certainly looking fine today."

Gracie smiled. "He is fine, as far as I can tell. It's just that it's time for his checkup and shots."

Her cat gave no sign of understanding that last word, just arched upward against the gentle pressure of a friendly caress and gave a small, contented *meow* as he looked up into the doctor's face. The veterinarian continued talking gently to her patient, as well as to his owner, even when Gracie was bold enough to approach the subject already discussed with her uncle.

"Oh, I don't think so," was Dave's first response to the proposal. Still, she did listen to what Gracie had to say.

"It's not that I'm not interested in the well-being of our town," she explained, after checking Gooseberry's heart and lungs and now feeling with her trained fingers all over his compliant body.

She kept her voice and manner equally calm and gentle as she added, "I'm one of the few people who regularly attend council meetings, and I've been able to have input on a number of topics—but I've never coveted more involvement than I have already as a private citizen."

Gracie pointed out that the current trio of candidates was less than thrilling, and Davena sighed. "Scary, isn't it, having only those guys running for our town's top job? And it surely is time for Tom to let someone new have a shot at it—I agree."

Gracie grinned at her. *Scary*—that's the same word I used just yesterday."

"You know what they say about great minds thinking the same thoughts," the vet said, laughing. "However, it always sounds like conceit when I'm the one to say it!"

Uncle Miltie was sitting on the porch, waiting for his niece to return. "How'd you make out?"

"Cat—fine. Mayoral race—uncertain."

"She didn't give a definite, final no?"

"Not yet, anyway."

"Well, that leaves room for hope, doesn't it?"

"It does. I'd known she likes to attend council meetings, but, in fact, it seems she's almost always there, and that she doesn't mind speaking up. It wouldn't surprise me if some members found her a little too involved, a little too much the concerned citizen."

"I'm getting more and more fond of that girl!"

"Me, too."

And it was the truth.

It was early evening when Gracie's niece Carter Stephens called from Chicago. After a few minutes of small talk Gracie asked, "Have you been speaking with your cousin recently?" It was possible that Arlen, worried about his mother, had given Carter a briefing on the situation in Willow Bend as he understood it.

"Guilty as charged!" She laughed. "He called me after he had talked to you."

"Was he asking you to talk me out of any possible desire I might have to run for mayor?"

"No, not if you really wanted the job—which, by the way, he assumes you don't. He's more concerned about this spate of rumors that's got you upset."

Gracie filled Carter in on her conversations with Rocky and with Herb, both of whom her niece knew well from her many visits to Willow Bend.

"I tell myself it's foolish to fret about what people are saying in a small town like this. Since everyone pretty much knows everyone else and their business, there's always talk about some thing or some one. The problem is, this time it's about Elmo Parks's reputation and that's one subject about which I have very strong feelings!"

"You still don't know what's being said?"

"Not yet." Gracie wasn't even sure whether to pray for more complete information. On the one hand, she was eager to get to the bottom of this, while on the other, she was afraid of what she might hear and how angry it would make her.

They talked for at least ten more minutes before Carter

said, "I'd better get off the phone. I'm expecting my date any time now."

"My goodness! Is this someone special?"

"Probably not in the sense you mean. But I do like his sense of humor, and he's been awfully fun to be with. Don't worry, I'll keep you posted!"

Gracie sighed as she hung up the phone. She had never quite given up hope that one day Carter and Pastor Paul might begin to know one another better. She obviously enjoyed his company every time she visited, but Carter was able, as far as Gracie could tell, to see the young minister only as a friend.

Who could tell what the future held?

Gracie awoke just after midnight, but she was so restless that Gooseberry finally left the bed and went to find himself a more satisfactory place to spend the night's last hours.

She turned on the light and looked over the books and magazines beside her bed. Deciding to get an early start by reading the *Daily Guideposts* devotion-for-the-day, she found, as she so often had, a special aptness for the current situation.

Looking in the back of the volume, she checked out the biographical information about the author of this particular passage and found that it was a Canadian. It seemed that this man and his wife had been very concerned about the school their children were attending. They had gone to all the parent-teacher meetings to stay in touch with what was happening.

However, finding themselves dismayed by some of the school board's decisions, the father finally had decided to run for one of the school board's open slots—and won! He wrote in the daily devotion of his determination to make a difference and of the gratitude he felt at having a chance to serve.

I do hope, God, that my appreciation of his determination to make a difference is the message I was to take away from this—and nothing more. I really can't see me as a mayor of anywhere. Can You?

G RACIE TURNED OFF THE LIGHT and lay down quietly on the bed, willing herself to go to sleep. It must have finally worked, for the next thing she was aware of was her cat using his paw to gently lift the sheet half-covering her head.

Gracie opened an eye, and saw his topaz-colored one only a couple of inches from hers. "You look like you're smiling, you rascal," she told him, rolling over and reaching to pet him. "And it is time for me to awaken, so I won't scold you— not that there'd be any point in that, anyway."

She didn't apologize for her yawn, either. She just pushed back the covers. "By the time I put on jeans and a shirt and have a cup of tea, Gooseberry, it will be plenty light enough for us to go for our walk."

This time, as they headed past the ball field and bleachers

Pastor Paul recently had mentioned, Gracie and Gooseberry stopped in front of the swings. She even considered the possibility of swinging for a little while—something she hadn't done for ages.

She decided not to, not because it was unseemly for a woman in her sixties, but because the dew on the seat would soak through her jeans. What good times she'd had here with Elmo and Arlen! Spur-of-the-moment picnics and Sunday school outings or at the rousing community picnic Elmo had instituted during his first year as mayor were all part of her memories.

You always had so many good ideas, Elmo—and that was another especially fine one. It was a fun time for people of all walks of life! We played games and sat around visiting and had a wonderful time together. And we usually ended up having a ball game, with men and women out there doing their very best, yet not minding too much if they or their teammates goofed up!

Now they'd come to the far side of the park, beyond which was what was still called by the old-timers the Julius Norton Fairweather Mansion, though it had been converted several years earlier into a home for a number of senior citizens.

Gooseberry started across its large, well-manicured lawn but, when Gracie called to him and started walking in the other direction, he rather reluctantly followed. It annoyed her that people had thrown these paper cups and plates on the ground, so she picked them up and carried them to a nearby trash-can. She and her companion then left the park by the exit onto the street perpendicular to the one where they'd entered.

Proceeding to the next block, they entered Abe's Deli. "Good morning, my friend!" she greeted Abe. "I'm about to ask a favor of you."

"Any request by you is honored here," he assured her.

She explained. "I came without my wallet this morning, and suddenly have a great desire for a just-baked-treat before heading home. Can I give you an I.O.U.?"

Laughing, he listed for her what was fresh that morning. "And if you won't expire before then, in about six minutes I'll be taking from the oven a plum cake. Might I inveigle you into being my official taster for this item?"

"*Ah*, yes—I'd be honored to take on that responsibility."

"So it's a deal!" He winked. "I don't pay you for your expertise and you don't pay me for the plum cake—nor for the extra two slices I send home with you."

Gracie cocked her head. "What an astute businessman you are, Abraham Levi Wasserman, giving away the store, practically, to a temporary moocher like me!"

He responded more seriously, "You are such a blessing, Gracie, to me and to most of Willow Bend! I couldn't repay you for your friendship were I to present you with an entire plum orchard plus the contents of my display case!"

She gave him a quick hug, broken immediately as she

realized that a woman and teen-aged boy were crossing the street and heading her way. Abe started back around the counter, but called a greeting to Jessica Larson and her son Jeffrey as they walked through the deli's door.

"Hi, Jessica!" Gracie said, seating herself on one of the counter seats. "Hi, Jeffrey!"

"Hello, Gracie! Abe!" Jessica looked as bossy as she always did. Jeffrey hung back. "I'm in a hurry, but I just need some bagels to take home."

"Cinnamon buns, too," Jeffrey put in.

"Not those," she stated firmly. "You'll get your hands all sticky and the car will be a major mess!"

"I'll be careful. . . "

His mother shook her head firmly. "You heard me!"

"But . . ."

"Now stop it, or you won't even get a bagel!"

Gracie felt embarrassed for the youth. She knew he was bright, especially when it came to putting things together or making things work. He had a mechanical bent. It was a shame Jessica so dominated his life—but everyone knew that her husband received much the same treatment.

"Is that the plum cake you were telling me about, Abe?" Gracie asked, seeing him start to remove a large baking sheet from the oven.

"It most certainly is."

"Looks delicious."

He tried to hide his pleasure at her approval. Jessica tossed her head. "None of that for us! People nowadays eat way too much sweet stuff, far more than's good for them.

"That's why I'm getting only plain bagels," she added, as Abe put the last of her order into a bag.

Gracie saw Jeffrey practically drooling over the sight and smell of the plum cake, so she asked, "Would you like a slice? I'm eating some here, as you see, and taking a bit home for Uncle Miltie. I have enough to share."

His eyes sparkled. Then he sighed. Jessica said coldly, "*Please*, Gracie! You heard me say he couldn't have any!"

Sliding off her stool, Gracie started for the door. "Sorry, Jessica," she said quietly. "I didn't mean to offend you."

Jeffrey whispered, "Thanks, anyway," as she passed him.

Uncle Miltie heartily approved of the plum cake and called Abe to tell him so.

"I hope you're being honest with me," was Abe's response. "Maybe your niece put you up to this. After all, she got her plum cake for free, and she probably thinks you all have to stay on my good side!"

"Hey! That reminds me! I heard about a man who claims he can't sit down and he can't stand up."

"Yes...?" prompted Abe.

"Well, if he tells the truth, he lies!"

Abe quietly hung up.

Marge stopped in on her way home from her store. She'd been unpacking new stock all day. "I have some great little beaded bags—there's one with a cat's face that could practically be Gooseberry's cousin!"

This reminded Marge of the double-birthday party Gracie had been asked to cater. "Have Bill and John told you yet what they want? Or how many people are invited?"

Gracie shook her head. "Nope—but they'd better soon! I can't go any further without their input."

"Can't you just call one of them?" Marge suggested. "The birthday is soon, isn't it?"

"Bill's and John's?" Uncle Miltie asked, coming in on the conversation.

"It's Tyne's and Tish's," Gracie explained. "Their husbands are throwing a surprise dinner for them."

He chuckled. "They're pretty dedicated to this twin thing, still wearing identical dresses and coats and shoes—even driving the same cars!"

"It must have seemed cute to their mom when they were little," Marge suggested, "but don't you wonder what their husbands think of it?"

"They must not mind. They've been married all this time! They got hitched in the same service for that matter—and I've neither seen nor heard anything to indicate that the guys find it strange or feel resentful."

"Amazing!"

"Yes, it is." But Gracie returned to the subject of the party. "Since it's meant to be a surprise, I've hesitated to phone either man at home, for fear I'd get one of the twins. Perhaps I can reach John at the Gas-and-Go...."

This, however, proved to be less satisfactory than she'd hoped. The mechanic listened to the options being offered but apparently had no idea yet as to how many guests were invited nor how many had said they'd come. He finally promised to get hold of Bill, assuring her one of them would call Gracie in the morning.

She sighed as she hung up. Uncle Miltie's expression showed that he recognized that the conversation hadn't helped. "What do you want to bet they decide on just having a tureen dinner? That way they don't have to decide anything!"

"I hadn't considered that possibility but," she sighed, "come to think of it, that might be best under this circumstance. It would mean I could share the responsibility with everyone else and stop having to badger Bill and John about decisions!"

"But how could you arrange a 'surprise' tureen dinner?"

"It's unusual," she admitted, shrugging broadly. "But we'd figure it out. I'm sure we could distract Tish and Tyne from the beginnings of any suspicion...."

Uncle Miltie patted his niece's arm. "That's one of the things I marvel at about you—your flexibility!"

"Thanks! But if you're working with people, it's totally necessary."

Marge nodded. "It's true in my business, too."

"Listen, girls," Uncle Miltie now said, "I was wondering if you, by any chance, knew the exact relation of a doorstep to a doormat?"

"Well, I won't ask how this fits with what we were talking about, but I give up." Gracie looked quizzically at her uncle. Marge did likewise.

Uncle Miltie chuckled. "It's a step-farther."

When she'd heard nothing from the brothers-in-law by the next morning, she again called John at the Gas-and-Go, asking what decisions they'd come to.

"Well, I—uh—we're still not sure what's best."

"How many people are invited?"

"I think around thirty."

"And how many people would that involve? Husbands and wives? Children? Distant relatives? Neighbors...?"

"Gee, I don't know."

"Did you address them to 'Mr. and Mrs.'?"

"Sure—some of them we did. But lots of people we just asked, like neighbors and friends at church."

"That's in addition to those thirty invitations you mailed?"

"*Ah-huh*—yeah. . . ."

"And did you keep track of those who said they'd be coming?"

"Well, not exactly."

Gracie waited.

"There's Jake and Mattie Cowper, our neighbors. And—and I suppose their youngest two. Their oldest kid's in college, so he probably won't come.

"And on the other side of us are the Kingstons. Judy said she was coming, but she wasn't sure about Stu, 'cause he has to go out of town on business and she doesn't know if he'll be back in time. And then there's the Knapps, and I suppose the youngest kid, Ron, will come."

"John?"

"Yeah?"

"Look, how about you and Bill sitting down with paper and pencil and figuring out exactly how many there will be. I really can't go out and arrange for purchases unless I know that. Plus, you haven't told me for sure which menu you want—the ham or stuffed chicken breast—or whatever."

"I like beef best."

"What about Bill? Is he okay with that?"

"I think so."

She laid her pen across the almost-unused paper before her. "I have a suggestion. Get together with Bill tonight—tomorrow morning at the very latest! Make out a complete list of the people you're pretty certain are coming. As I told you, there'll be a set charge for each meal that's prepared, so you don't want to pay me for twenty or thirty extras. At the same time, I need to be sure we won't run out of food, either."

"Oh!"

"And I need to know for sure which meat both of you decide upon, as well as which side dishes you want, and what salads and breads. And I don't even know if you'd like something else in addition to one huge birthday cake or what... "

"Gracie?"

"Yes, John?"

"Look, I—don't know anything about any of this."

"Do you think Bill might?"

"I—sort of doubt it. Don't you?"

She remembered what she and Uncle Miltie had recently discussed and suddenly decided to mention it. "There's one other possibility. If you guys can't come up with specifics, then maybe my catering it isn't the best idea."

"What else are you thinking about?"

"Your wives have been wonderful, much-loved choir members for years, and I'll bet everyone would help if you were to ask them to help out with a tureen dinner."

"Gosh."

"It's not that I don't want to do the catering," she started to explain.

He asked anxiously, "You think they actually might do it?"

"I can't speak for them, of course, but I rather think so.

Everyone knows how Tish and Tyne are always pitching in."

"They do, that's right."

"When you talk to Bill, just mention this as a possibility. If he thinks it's a good idea, we can start in on the general assignments right away . . . and let the gang organize the specifics, according to what they sign up for."

John called back in less than a half-hour to report that both he and Bill would be thrilled if the choir would handle the party. The invitations had been mailed and had even said that the party would be at the Family Activity Center at Eternal Hope a week from Sunday.

Gracie spent part of the morning contacting the choir members she could most count on. But she knew that, in the end, everyone would come through.

At lunch, Uncle Miltie was beaming at her. "Well done, Gracie! You've turned this into a loving project, with the twins' good friends all signing on. I could hear your end of a couple of the conversations."

He made a thumbs-up.

"You're right. That's the kind of community this is."

"I'd have enjoyed catering a really nice dinner for the twins," she told him. "But you know what, Uncle Miltie? I suspect they'll appreciate this sort of affair a whole lot more."

"I'm sure they will."

Her mind was going nonstop even as she did the dishes

after dinner, with Uncle Miltie drying. With eagerness she sat down at the table with the phone and a yellow legal tablet, the pages roughly divided into sections.

GUEST LIST was the first of these—but she was still in the dark on this score. For HELPERS, she jotted down the names of those she'd contacted thus far and what they'd offered to do—and started a separate column of those she'd still be checking with.

The next page was DECORATING. She was almost sure Marge would welcome that responsibility. She called Marge, and they discussed who'd be best at helping her. "What about Estelle?" Gracie asked.

"Oh, she'd be fine, of course—but she so often takes over anything she gets involved with—or she tries to, anyway."

"Might it help if you're made the official chairperson of that committee and she's your assistant?"

Marge chuckled. "Okay. That's good thinking."

"And she'll probably volunteer to sing 'Happy Birthday' solo," Gracie added.

"*Uh-oh!*"

"She'll be very eager to involve herself, that's for sure!"

"She prefers singing to cooking. Or should I say singing to just about anything? But I'm sure I can handle her when it comes to balloons."

"I get you! Make use of some of that breath control she's always bragging about!"

"You got it, Gracie my girl!"

"This is going to be fun," Gracie said.

"Anything we do together here in Willow Bend always is," Marge reminded her.

I T WAS ONE OF THOSE DAYS when Gracie wasn't sure what to wear. The thermometer outside the big kitchen window said fifty-seven degrees Fahrenheit, but there was a haze. It wasn't really gray, just blurry enough to let Gracie know that the sun might appear to turn things hotter at any minute.

Gracie was ready for a long walk, and she hoped Gooseberry was, too. They started off at a fast pace, but by the time they got to the outskirts of town they slowed somewhat. She watched her cat busily investigating the tall weeds and grasses alongside the road.

Suddenly she saw Gooseberry stop and stand perfectly still, staring into a stand of thistles and burdock. His head was cocked slightly, as though listening intently.

So Gracie did likewise.

"I—don't hear anything, Gooseberry, not even breezes

moving leaves." But the cat took a few more slow steps away from her, and Gracie followed. This time she thought there might be a tiny sound.

She was now close enough to look downward into the weeds and saw—what? It looked like a somewhat irregular ball of some scratchy something. But then it moved slightly, and she saw a tiny sparkle, two of them. Whatever it was, it was definitely alive and almost completely covered with burrs!

Gooseberry was moving nearer, and Gracie grabbed for him. "No, don't touch it with your nose or foot! No use getting all those nasty things stuck to you, as well."

Well, she couldn't just leave the poor creature—but she didn't have anything to protect her hands. It suddenly moved a little more, and Gracie could think of only one thing that might work. Removing the light jacket she'd tied around her waist, she started to slowly lower it over and around the animal. She'd worry about the stickers clinging to it later.

Tucking the jacket around and under it, she lifted her catch upward, to the accompaniment of a somewhat louder and more plaintive mewing. Gooseberry didn't seem at all pleased with this turn of events, even using his paw—claws extended—to pull at the material.

"Now stop that!" Gracie commanded, pushing him away even as she had to wonder what in the world she was going to do with her burden now that she'd "captured" it.

She soon found it was going to be heavy-going carrying

such a precariously wrapped bundle all the way home. The problem was she needed to hold it carefully away from her body, as some of the burrs were starting to attach themselves to her jeans.

She'd gone no more than a couple of hundred paces back toward Willow Bend when she heard a vehicle behind her. Turning, she realized with relief that it was Lester Twomley's pickup.

"Thank You, Lord!" she murmured, just standing there until her friend came abreast of her and stopped.

He rolled down the window to ask, "Are you okay?"

She nodded. "Gooseberry and I are, but this little fellow isn't."

Lester raised an eyebrow.

"I'll explain in a minute. But could you maybe drive us home? I'll know better what to do once I've examined what I'm carrying here."

Les's eyebrow climbed a fraction higher. But he reassured her, "Your rescue mission now has an accomplice—just climb up! You, too, Gooseberry."

As she fastened her seatbelt, she said, "It's going to be an awful job getting all those burrs off of it—that's already pretty obvious."

The truck moved forward as he interrupted with, "If you think it's really going to be that painful for the animal, might you want me to take you directly to the vet's?"

"I—don't know what's best. And I came out without my cell phone."

"Here, use mine."

He handed it to her, but she shook her head. "I don't know Davena's number, do you?"

"I'm afraid not."

"Well then, how about just dropping me off at her office? If she can't see us, I guess I'll have to carry this poor little creature home with me, and Uncle Miltie and I will do the best we can."

His tone was a little troubled. "I'd feel a whole lot more comfortable about this whole situation if I knew for sure it's a cat wrapped up in your coat."

As if on cue, a tiny mew issued forth from her bundle. "Don't you agree it sounds like a kitten?"

"Sure does."

Within a few minutes they were parked in front of the office, with Les insisting that he accompany her. He wanted to make sure everything was all right before heading off, he told her.

There were already two people in the waiting room with their dogs. Spotting Gracie and Gooseberry, Annie—the young woman who'd assisted Dr. Wilkins ever since she'd opened her All Creatures Small animal clinic—immediately asked, "Something wrong with Gooseberry today?"

Gracie shook her head. "It's quite a different problem this time—one which perhaps I should be taking to the SPCA."

"Oh? What's in there?" Annie had just realized Gracie was carrying a covered bundle.

"I think it's a kitten."

"But you're not sure?"

"I found it out on the Avery Road or, rather, Gooseberry found it."

"Well, let's have a look," Annie said, coming toward them. Gracie leaned over to set her jacket gently on the floor. She opened it enough for both Annie and Les to look inside.

"No wonder you couldn't tell!"

And Les breathed a soft, "The poor little thing!"

Gracie held Gooseberry back with her other hand. "I was going to take it home and put on my garden gloves to pull off these burrs, but I was afraid that might hurt it unbearably. Do you suppose Davena—Dr. Wilkins—could maybe give it something to help with the pain while the stickers get extracted?"

The dog owners were staring at the mystery animal. Annie said to them, "As you know, we don't ever like to take patients out-of-turn. But an emergency situation's different. Would either of you mind terribly if we have the doctor see this one first?"

The dog owners shook their heads.

Les asked as he started to follow Annie and Gracie into one of the examining rooms, "Do you think Dr. Wilkins would mind if I got my camera and took a few pictures? I've never in my life seen this many burrs stuck on anything!"

"I'm sure it's okay," Annie said, "though it would be best to wait till you ask her permission."

He was back within a minute, and snapped a couple of digital shots as soon as Davena Wilkins joined them and gave him the go-ahead. She agreed it would be necessary to anesthetize the patient to facilitate the burr removal.

Gooseberry was pacing and rubbing against Gracie, obviously upset by the little *meows* of pain and fear. Gracie understood—she felt the same way herself. With gloves supplied by Annie, she held the kitten, which Davena estimated to be little more than six or eight weeks old. It was turning out to be entirely black except for its white feet and a small white bib.

All in all, the procedure took less time than Gracie had anticipated. However, an important issue remained: what would become of the kitten now that it was freed of its burdock overcoat?

Gracie thought a moment. "You know what, Les? These pictures of yours might make a good feature for Rocky. This way, people will be reminded how cruel it can be to just throw helpless little animals like this out of a car!"

"He's welcome to use them. It would be worth it if it kept even one kitten or puppy from going through what this one has!"

The veterinarian, plucking off a few final sharp bits, murmured, "Also, if nobody comes forward to claim her as his own, maybe a photo-spread might induce some soft-hearted reader to offer her a home. She's really a beautiful kitten, and friendly, and would probably make a good pet."

Gracie picked up the kitten, snuggling the tiny body against her cheek. She then put it back down and stroked Gooseberry. His back was still raised, indicating his mistrust of the proceedings.

"Don't worry, old guy, you're not about to have any competition at home."

Annie had set a bowl of milk on the floor, and everyone was delighted to see the thin little kitten eagerly lap it up.

Turning back toward the vet, Gracie asked, "If I were to pay her board, would you keep her here for a few days, Davena, until her owner's found? Or someone who wants her?"

The doctor gave a sad smile. "I'd be happy to, Gracie—but you should be aware that it's highly unlikely that there's an owner who wants her. When whoever it is reads the paper and realizes how much time we put into working with this patient, all that person's really going to be seeing is dollar signs."

"Oh, I hadn't thought of that."

"But that doesn't mean someone else may not ask to adopt her."

As Gracie went back outside with Les, she asked him if he could spare a few more minutes. Would he stop with her and show Rocky the pictures?

He grinned. "I'm already late getting to my next job. But

you know my weaknesses all too well . . . photography and animals. I'll just make a quick call"—he was already punching in numbers—"so they know I'm detained but intend to be there soon."

At his office, Rocky stood in the doorway to greet them. "Hi, what's up? Les, you don't usually accompany Gracie here. She just plagues us all on her own!"

Gracie filled him in on her plan. Seeing that he looked skeptical, she paused. She put her hands on her hips and stared at him sternly until he mock-cowered in front of her.

"Okay! Okay!" he protested. "Let's just agree I'm not a kitten kind of guy!"

"You have a heart as soft as that kitten's fur, you just don't like admitting it. The poor thing certainly would have died had Gooseberry and I not found it, and if Davena hadn't helped."

"You've made your point, Gracie. And I won't scream character assassination! And you, Les, have some handsome shots here. Would you permit me to use some of these—with one-time rights only, of course—giving you publishing credit for them?"

"Sure. That's why we're here."

"And," Gracie added, "aside from finding a good home for a beautiful little black-and-white kitten—what about giving Davena Wilkens, Doctor of Veterinary Medicine, an editorial plug? You know, 'if we only had more like her,' and so on?"

He burst out laughing. "It's you, Gracie, that we need more of, but if I wrote that, you'd have my scalp, maybe even roll me in the burdock patch! Still, I'll do whatever you say, and that means praising Dave Wilkins to the skies and then some!"

Gracie tried to look stern but failed. "Anything to stop me from plaguing you, I guess. Why did I ever think you seemed to welcome my drop-ins?"

Rocky held up his hands in protest, and they all began laughing. "That kitten didn't know she'd be making head-lines!" he told Gracie and Les.

Bill Anderson, Tyne's husband, called that afternoon. "Hey, Gracie, John and I would like to change the time of the party from late afternoon to right after church."

"I hope there's an awfully good reason for your wanting to do that. I've already talked over all the arrangements with the choir."

"We did think five o'clock was best, but it seems our in-laws have a conflict—they've got to be in Chicago for some-thing that evening. You know, Tyne and Tish would hate it if their folks weren't here."

Gracie sighed, then hoped Bill hadn't heard it and thought she was being difficult.

"It's just that it would be impossible to keep it a surprise that way, Bill. The choir members have to be in the loft not

only to sing their anthem but also to lead in the congrega-
tional singing.

"If everyone but Tyne and Tish were to get up and leave in
order to have the meal ready as the service was ending, it
would be awfully strange. What would they think, sitting
there alone?"

"Well, maybe we could make it just a little later—you
know, 12:30 instead of at noon?"

Give me strength, Lord—they're asking the impossible! "They'll
know something's up if everyone but themselves arrives that
morning with bowls and casseroles!"

"Well, maybe it won't hurt too much if during church they
get some little hint. . . ."

She somehow controlled the next sigh, which threatened to
be the biggest one yet. "I honestly wish there was a way of
making this work." She thought for a moment. "Have you
found out exactly when the Turners have to leave?"

"Not specifically. I just know they have tickets to something in the early evening."

"When did you find out about it?"

"Just a little while ago."

Well, she would try one more suggestion: "Could you get
hold of them and explain our difficulty in rescheduling? See if
they might be willing to forego this one event—or, if not,
would they be able to stop by, at least, at the party if it were

moved up even an hour or hour and a half—to three-thirty or four o'clock?"

"You think that might work out better?"

"Not as well as at the time you'd indicated on the invitations —which reminds me of all those phone calls you and John will have to take care of in order to get the word out to everyone you've invited. At least, in that way, you'll also find out who can't make it. And who can."

She heard a sigh now from her caller. He moaned, "I sure hope John has a full list!"

"Me, too! Anyway, I'll need to hear from you by tonight, Bill. This rescheduling may mean that some of the helpers I've lined up might need to change things, too."

"And," she added, "I obviously can't count on four of my usual stalwarts—the birthday twins and their spouses!"

Uncle Miltie came in from an afternoon at the senior center. He had the usual tidbits of local news to relay.

Only one fully caught her attention: "The guys were reminiscing again about the good old days, decades before I came to Willow Bend. There were a lot of real characters back then, like that fellow at the library who came in every day, rain or shine, and insisted on sweeping the entire place."

"I remember Benny Jacobs well," she told him. "Keeping that library spotless was his mission in life. I doubt that he, himself, was ever able to read anything more advanced than a picture book, but Abbie—the librarian who retired just before you came—once said to me, 'Bennie makes things shine around here and I think even the books appreciate it.'"

"Did anyone try to teach him to read?"

She nodded. "Several of us offered, but he showed no interest. He liked what he did best—the library maintenance—and he liked to talk to folks. That was all."

"What happened to him?"

She frowned. "He was killed by a hit-and-run driver late one night, right there by his beloved *liberry* as he called it."

"He worked at night?"

"Not usually—and it was raining the night it happened. His mother said she thought he'd gone to bed, and was dumbfounded when Syd Browning, the chief of police at the time, came to her door and told her Bennie was dead."

"Did they catch whoever was responsible?"

"They never did—which made Elmo angry."

"I guess, though, that happens lots of times."

"But it does seem especially tragic when it happens to one of this world's innocents. Had Bennie been a banker's son or the chairman of the school board, Elmo felt much more attention would have been given to the investigation."

"But maybe...," Uncle Miltie began, then changed that to, "well, I wasn't here then."

"No, you weren't."

And as she passed his chair on the way to the refrigerator,

she slid her hand across his shoulders, an expression of gratitude for his presence. He couldn't be her husband, but he was her uncle, and they were a team.

"Thanks for everything," she said to him softly.

"Oh, my dear, thank you."

RLEN AND LITTLE ELMO arrived shortly before she and Uncle Miltie were ready for bed on Friday night. "*Surprise*, Gramma!" her grandson shouted, barging in through the kitchen door.

She practically flew from her recliner and ran to meet him and his father. "And what a wonderful one it is!" she cried, lifting the little boy off his feet and gathering him in her arms.

"We've been drivin' and drivin'," he announced. "I got out of school real early, before lunch even. Daddy came for me, and we've been drivin' ever since!"

She looked over his head. "Oh, Arlen, it's so great to have you both here!"

He held up the key with which he'd unlocked the door. "You gave me this eons ago, and I figured it was time to see if it worked." He came to her, long arms encircling this woman he loved so much. "I found myself worrying far too much about you, Mom, so thought we'd come make sure you're okay." His son watched them impatiently.

"It's a slight reversal of roles, isn't it? Not so very long ago, I used to fret about you, your whereabouts and well-being, all the time!"

He laughed. "And I thought your apron strings much too short, and very much too tight."

Little Elmo thought about this. "Do you wear aprons, Gramma?"

"I used to, dear, a long time ago. But not so much these days." She reached down to hug him again. "You did stop to eat, didn't you?"

"Yeah," the youngster informed her. "I got french fries and a hamburger first—then an ice cream cone later."

"But that was half-way across Ohio," his father informed her. "After a good long nap."

"So you're both ready for real food," she deduced. "Follow me to the kitchen—I might even find an apron to tie on!"

They were still at the table when there were footsteps on the porch and a knock on the door. "Come on in, whoever it is!" Gracie called out. "I'm frozen in place!"

A second later, Rocky entered the kitchen. "I was driving past and saw that New York license plate. Thought I'd stop a minute and welcome you back to Willow Bend. It must be a surprise visit since your mother never mentioned it, and, believe me, she'd consider it front-page news!"

"Rocky, it's great to see you!" Arlen exclaimed warmly.

Gracie thought to ask, "I'm sure you've eaten something by now, but how about some vegetable soup before joining us for cherry cobbler?"

"You won't get an argument from me!" He stopped at the kitchen sink and reached for the bottle of dish detergent, as he always did. "I'll just wash my hands and be ready."

He asked Arlen how long it had taken them to get here and why he hadn't just hopped on a plane. The younger man explained, "I don't get the chance to do much long-distance driving anymore, and I just love the scenery in Pennsylvania and Ohio and through this much of Indiana.

"Besides, with getting to the airport and doing all the waiting at that end, then having the hassle at Chicago and renting a car and driving here—well, it was a no-brainer for Elmo and me to decide on driving this time."

They continued sitting around the table until the little boy yawned for perhaps the fourth time in five minutes and his grandmother suggested, "Let's you and me go upstairs and get ready for bed, dear. Would you like to sleep in the room you ordinarily use, or with your dad?"

He looked across at his father. "Can I sleep with you?"

"Sure, son. I'll be upstairs in just a little while."

Picking up the boy's small knapsack, Gracie took it to his room upstairs and stayed with him as he prepared for bed. She read two of his favorite books before stopping for prayer-time, then kissed him goodnight, saying what she'd nightly repeated to Arlen as a child, "Goodnight, my sleepy darling. See you in God's morning."

The only response was a tiny snore—a snore-let, really.

The three men were engrossed in their conversation when she walked back into the kitchen. Rocky was saying, ". . . and we've made almost no progress, finding out who's starting this stuff or why."

Uncle Miltie put in, "Nor what's actually being said, for that matter. Gracie says it's like fighting a fog—your punches just go right through it."

"It's funny that it's all come up at the same time the may-oral race is getting under way."

Arlen said, "You're not planning to run, are you, Mom?"

She shrugged. "Probably not. . . "

"Probably?"

"Well, Dave—Davena Wilkins, that is—hasn't agreed to do it—but I'm still hoping she will. I therefore see no point in making my possible candidacy a topic of conversation."

They'd long since finished the cobbler when Uncle Miltie glanced at the clock and grumbled, "If you're not going to go home at a reasonable hour, Mr. Editor, I might just as well challenge you to a game of Scrabble."

Rocky pushed back his chair. "Okay, I'm out of here! If he beats me one more time with some impossible-seeming seven-letter word, I'll be forced to move away in disgrace!"

The younger man laughed. "I suspect I may have cut my baby teeth on those wooden squares!"

Gracie smiled at her only child. "And it undoubtedly helped you win all those regional spelling bees year after year."

All of them went out to the porch to see Rocky on his way.

"Goodnight, Arlen! Welcome home again!" he called back at them. "I'm sure you're too excited to sleep, Gracie, but you need your rest if you're going to keep pace with little El!"

He roared off into the night.

"He's a good man," Arlen said. "But his muffler needs work!"

"Until he does get it fixed, it's like belling a cat. I know when he's coming . . . or going!" Gracie said, laughing.

Her uncle, however, grumbled, "If he just weren't so blamed opinionated!"

His niece and great-nephew both bit their lips.

"It's not funny!"

Arlen put a hand on Uncle Miltie's arm. "It's just that the two of you are so very much alike."

Gooseberry wasn't on her bed when Gracie awoke early the next morning, but she wasn't surprised. As she crept quietly into the room where her grandson was sleeping, she found her cat where she expected to see him—tucked against little Elmo's legs.

Even when she headed downstairs, Gooseberry stayed put. She caught herself thinking, Oh, ye of fickle loyalties! But the smile remained on her face.

Good morning, God. I just want to thank You again for providing me with such splendid people in my life! I don't know how I'd ever manage without their special varieties of love—all my relatives and friends, and even Gooseberry.

How did the often difficult and demanding Miles Stevens survive on his own? Or Jessica Larson, who had so few close friends? Or Harvey Smith? Or Tony Randolph? *I know I shouldn't leap to judgment, Lord, but I never see any of these people seeming to be happy or fulfilled or aware of Your love. Not like I am. Oh, how I wish they could be!*

Taking a bag of blueberries from the freezer, she mixed up a batch of muffins. Undoubtedly it was the aroma emanating from the oven that brought both her son and uncle into the kitchen just as she took out the two pans with their perfectly raised and browned contents.

Arlen almost burned his fingers when removing the paper baking cup from the muffin he had grabbed with such delight. It didn't stop him from nibbling off a bite, however— and he exhaled loudly with pleasure, as well as a few crumbs. "Wow!" he said, wiping his mouth, "these are not from a mix!"

"The exact recipe you remember! Only the ingredients are fresh!" his mother assured him.

Uncle Miltie now had a bright idea, "Let's give your mother a cheer! *Hooray* for Gracie! *Hooray* for Gracie! *Hip! Hip!* More muffins, *yay!*"

Arlen, the crumbs from a second muffin now on his mouth, echoed his uncle. "*Hooray*, Mom the muffin maker! *Yay!*"

Gracie scolded them, "You'll wake little Elmo, but, of course, your loud—very loud—approval is entirely pleasing to this old cook and cateress!"

Arlen said in a whisper to his uncle, "You know how to keep them coming, don't you? What does it take to get a couple of apple pies and a German chocolate cake?"

Gracie said, "I heard that and, yes, it's his utterly shameless flattery that keeps him in calories."

All three affectionately laughed. Then Gracie changed the subject. "I know you're planning to stay only until Monday, just two days from now, so what would you like to do, or whom, exactly, do you want to see?"

"First of all, I think I need to talk with Herb. Is tomorrow morning, right now, an okay time?"

Uncle Miltie nodded. "I think so."

Gracie, however, went right over to the phone and called the police station. Gladys Martin answered and, when Gracie said she'd not expected to hear her voice that early in the day,

Gladys said she'd traded with one of the other women since she'd taken her mother to Chicago on Wednesday.

"So what can I help you with, Gracie?"

"Herb's not there, is he?"

"Hold on. He was, though I think he may have headed out."

Gracie waited, then heard Herb's deep voice saying, "Hi, Gracie. You caught me just as I was leaving."

"Sorry to hold you up, but Arlen arrived unexpectedly last evening and leaves again day after tomorrow. Any chance he might see you before then?"

"Is he there now?"

Her answer was to hold the phone out to her son. "Herb'd like to speak to you."

"Hi, Herb. . . Well, yes, I'll have to admit that's the case. From a distance, we couldn't figure out what was going on. . . Oh, you, too? Well . . . sure, that'd be great."

He put the phone down, saying, "Well, Mom, you're going to get rid of some more of those muffins in just a couple of minutes."

She laughed. "I wasn't worried! Between you and your uncle, and Rocky—and little Elmo—I expect to be baking steadily between now and Monday."

Soon Herb, too, was comfortably covered in muffin crumbs as he discussed the rumor situation with the late Elmo Parks' family.

"As far as I've determined, what's being said is mostly that he didn't do enough—that your dad didn't care about the people or the town—that he was too conscious of building his own image—that sort of thing."

It was all Gracie could do to keep from interrupting and launching into a long detailed list of all the accomplishments Elmo Parks had chalked up and how uninterested in self-promotion he had always been. However, she cautioned herself against grabbing the floor when, in fact, she'd only be preaching to the converted. Uncle Miltie, Herb Bower, and, above all, her son were all already on her side.

Then, too, she was learning some new information, and she didn't want to distract Herb from going on.

Arlen asked, "Are other people coming to you, complaining or wondering what this is all about?"

"I wish they were! But no crime, really, is being committed. Anyone who knew Elmo Parks cares about him as one of the best men they ever knew, so, if those folks hear the rumors, they just ignore them, anyway."

"But what about those people who didn't know him, or even those who did and might be willing to believe ill of him?"

Herb shrugged. "I'm not sure. If the motivation has something to do with the upcoming election, it's just got larger implications."

"But Dad's gone—and Mom's not running for office."

Herb looked at Gracie. He cocked an eyebrow. "Well, Gracie?"

"I've never, ever said I'd run. Never. Ever."

He persisted, "And have you ever stated firmly, incontrovertibly that you wouldn't?"

"I'm trying to get Davena to throw her stethoscope into the ring, but if she doesn't and there's nobody better than those three now out there, I may have to, with a 'write-in campaign.'"

"So," Herb thought out loud, "it seems to me, Arlen, as if there's at least some possibility all this is aimed at your mom, either to discourage her from running or else to keep people from voting for her if her late husband did such a lousy job."

"Which is a downright lie!" Uncle Miltie declared furiously. It mattered little that he was the one person in this room who'd not lived in Willow Bend at the time.

Arlen wondered, "What about Tony and Harvey? I'll confess to not remembering much about either of them."

"Someone recently referred to those two as not being 'viable candidates,' despite the fact that they seem to like running. Normally I'd agree with that—but our Tom Ritter has been a disappointment to even those who voted for him. He's smart enough and has even done a fair job, but his better-than-you manner and his wife's airs have simply turned off most people."

"So where does that leave the community?"

"Good question. It does make your mother look to be a grand and glorious choice, if only she had the political ambition. Playing on her sympathies is no way to get us a fully engaged mayor, I'd say. I believe her—alas—that she's truly against the idea of running for office."

"Thank you, Herb," Gracie said.

The phone rang and Herb, the closest, lifted the receiver and handed it to Gracie, who answered, "Hello?"

"Hello, Gracie." It was Barb, sounding upset, as she so often did. "Did you hear that Amy has a bad cold, and that she may not be able to sing with us tomorrow?"

"Oh, I'm sorry."

"I just don't know if we can sing our anthem without her. You know she has a solo part."

"Does she think she won't be able to do it?"

"She doesn't sound like she can."

"Did she call you about it?"

There was a drawn-out exhalation. "She didn't have to! I stopped in at Abe's and she was working there, as she always does Saturday mornings. She sounded terrible!"

"Is she coughing or sneezing or anything?"

"No, just had a croak every time she opened her mouth. I honestly thought Abe should have sent her home."

"Well, I suspect she feels she can do it if she didn't tell you otherwise," Gracie said reassuringly. "Amy never lets us down with no warning."

"But if she can't at the last moment, we'll be in an awful fix!" Barb had a tendency to seek out worries where only budding concerns were making themselves known.

"We'll make out fine, Barb. Should we discover that's the case when we get to church, Estelle can pick up that short solo part—or Les or another of the tenors can master it quickly enough."

"But what if someone else comes down with something, too?"

Dear Lord, why is this otherwise wonderful person so determined to make herself miserable? "Please, dear, just get some rest, you'll feel better after you do."

"But. . ."

"You're getting upset over something that's probably going to work out fine, Barb. How about making yourself a cup of tea, then sitting down to enjoy it while you read a book or watch some good TV show?"

There was the sound of a deep breath being drawn in. "I suppose you're right, Gracie, but I so hate not having our music go right!"

"It won't, dear."

"I do hope so!"

Arlen was sitting there shaking his head. "You have the patience of a saint!"

"Maybe on the outside." Gracie laughed. "But you can't see the nerves fraying on the inside!"

8

ELMO CAME DOWNSTAIRS right after that, the large orange cat close at his heels. "Can we go for a walk with Gooseberry, Gramma?"

"I was hoping you'd like to do that!"

"Right away?" He was already heading for the door.

"How about first eating one of these blueberry muffins and drinking some milk?"

Nodding, he reached for a muffin and started to peel off its paper exterior. "Sure." The muffins were cool now, and he whizzed through two before offering Gooseberry the last chunk of his second.

He was wearing the clothing they'd laid out the night before, blue shorts and red sneakers and a blue-and-white striped tee, and as they went out the door and started down the steps, holding hands, he said, "You have red shoes, too."

So she did! She'd chosen this pair, thinking of him and of the red sneakers Arlen had worn when he was a lad. Every time she put them on, she'd wish she had one of her boys by her side—and her prayer had been answered.

Gooseberry unhesitatingly turned right at the sidewalk and his humans followed along, chatting comfortably, not caring where they went as long as they were together. It was several blocks later that she realized he was probably heading for the park, where they didn't often go.

Recently, however, they had.

Might Gooseberry be smart enough to be heading for the swings? However, just before the swings came into view, before her grandson realized where they were headed, she had another thought.

She took tighter hold of Elmo's hand and called to get Gooseberry's attention as she turned left, which route would take them to the edge of town. "The last time I walked out this particular road I saw a very young calf in the field with its mother," she told him. "It must have been newly born, for it was still wobbly on its thin little legs."

He danced with excitement and tugged her along. "Let's go see it!"

As they walked along, she pointed out the redwing blackbird swooping by, and they stopped to watch a fat, grizzled groundhog not concerned in the least about these two-legged creatures gawking at him as he continued eating his weed-breakfast along the roadside.

"Why are they called groundhogs?"

"I'm not sure. They don't look much like pigs, do they? And, though they live in holes in the ground, a lot of other critters do, likewise. They're also called woodchucks, which makes even less sense."

She remembered something she thought he'd like. "When I was little, we used to have a tongue-twister that went like this, 'How much wood would a woodchuck chuck if a woodchuck could chuck wood?'"

He tried to repeat the words. "Let's say it together this time," she suggested, and they did it twice, slowly and carefully.

"That's not hard, Gramma."

"Well, then, let's go faster and faster," she challenged him.

"*Oops!*" he cried, as his tongue twisted around the words. The groundhog sped off, alarmed.

They kept walking slowly. The peaceful morning, with the birds in the trees and the clouds above them, thrilled Gracie as it always did. But to have little Elmo next to her meant God had truly read her heart.

As soon as they walked in the house, Elmo shared with Uncle Miltie his newly learned tongue twister, "...woodchuck could chuck wood!" he finished triumphantly.

His great-great-uncle laughed as he reached to rumple the boy's hair. "I used to love that, too."

"Such things," Gracie told them both, "are of no earthly use—of no practical use, I'd better say. The fun they give and the memories they stir up are what make them worthwhile."

Uncle Miltie now asked, "Tell me, did you get to hear the critter whistle?"

The little boy looked suspicious. "Groundhogs . . . whistle?"

"So they tell me, though I never did hear it myself," Uncle Miltie admitted. "I understand he does that when he gets perturbed, or scared, or something. Back when I was little, people sometimes referred to a groundhog as a 'whistle pig.'"

"Wow! He's got lots of names!"

"Yes, he does." And Uncle Miltie went on to tell of Pennsylvania's Punxatawney Phil, the most famous groundhog in the world. His trick was his supposed success at weather prognostication—the predicting of when spring will actually arrive in the Quaker State.

"Does he always get it right?"

Uncle Miltie laughed. "I'm afraid not—but his arrival is big business in that town, their biggest day in the year."

Gracie wondered if little Elmo understood what that reference to "biggest day" meant, but her grandson was more attuned to the animal itself, a subject with which her uncle was happy to remain. She did wonder where Arlen was, since his car was still out front, but Uncle Miltie said he'd left shortly after she did, saying he, also, needed to get out and walk.

He didn't return until she was peeling potatoes for the noon meal, and she was grateful that he immediately came over to give her a hug and kiss—like her Elmo used to do, even if coming into the kitchen for the tenth time during a day. This was one of the things she missed most even now, so long after that horrible accident, which had claimed his life.

What had caused it? That unwanted question kept popping into her mind at the most inconvenient times—as if there were ever a convenient time. Well, she was not going to permit it to stay there for another second! "Who did you get to see this morning, darling?" she asked her son.

"I went first to Miller's. Hammie was pretty busy with all those customers who have to wait till Saturdays to come in. But I did talk to him a little, as he was hefting feed sacks around and toting cases of dog food. I was glad, honestly, to see him so busy—it's such an old-fashioned place. It's great so many people want it to stay just like it is.

"Bud Smith was there. He took over as principal my last year. Any memories I have of him are pleasant, but brief. Then Phil Murphy arrived, and we talked old band gossip. I never was in it, as you well know, but I hung out with a lot of the horn section."

She smiled at him.

He went on, "I was about to leave when your Dr. Wilkins—Davena—drove in."

Gracie waited.

"She seems to be well liked."

"Very much so—and respected."

"Everyone wanted to talk with her, so it wasn't till she was about to leave that I grabbed a couple of her purchases and marched right along with her to her Jeep, introducing myself and saying how many good things I'd heard about her."

"And. . . ?"

He grinned. "She was friendly and curious. Anyway, I told her how much you were hoping she'd decide to run for mayor, but that I was acting entirely on my own in mentioning it to her."

"Thank you, dear. I don't want her thinking I'm putting on additional pressure.

"She doesn't seem to think she has the time and energy to do a really good job, that's the impression I got."

"Our present mayor sure doesn't give it much time and energy—unless it's an occasion when he's sure to get his picture in the paper!"

Arlen looked at her. "Rocky plays along?"

"Sometimes he can't avoid it, I guess. And it's more from a sense of civic duty than respect. If you want to know the truth, I accuse him of not choosing the most flattering shots of our mayor every chance he gets."

"Sneaky."

"Let's just say Rocky is versatile when it comes to his editorializing," Gracie remarked.

"Just like I said, sneaky." Arlen grinned at his mother. And Gracie smiled lovingly back.

During lunch Elmo attempted to teach his dad his tongue twister, which Gracie knew Arlen had learned as a child. Uncle Miltie offered some other classic ones, like "She sells sea shells down by the sea shore," and they were all still laughing as Gracie served them the bowl of fruit salad she'd cut up.

She saw her grandson yawn several times. But when he had finished eating, he told Gracie, "Time to go to the park, Gramma!"

"I thought you were headed there this morning," his father commented.

"I changed our route. And I'm glad I did. The tongue twisters inspired by seeing that woodchuck have certainly enlivened the day so far!"

Elmo slid his legs around to the side of his chair. "Let's go right now!"

"Just give me time to put what's left over in the fridge and the dishes in the dishwasher."

"I'll help!"

Arlen and Uncle Miltie were already ensconced in the

latter's workshop when Gracie and little Elmo left a few minutes later. Gooseberry was trotting after them. "Which things do you like best in the park, Elmo?"

"Everything—but that merry-go-round you have to run and push, then jump on is my fav'rite."

After excitedly settling himself on a swing, he held on tight with his hands and thrust his sturdy little legs out straight as he went forward, then tucked them under the wooden seat as he went back. "I do this back home, too!"

"I remember," Gracie said. "We had some fun times on your playground."

"Where'd Gooseberry go?" Elmo now asked.

"Who knows?" She looked around. "He's not far away, I'm sure, but maybe he saw a fat bug or something."

"Why does he chase bugs when he gets all that good food at your house?"

"It's fun for him, like the swings are for you. And it's part of a cat's nature."

"Does he eat them?" He wrinkled his nose at the thought of something so unappetizing.

"Sometimes he eats a bug, but often when he catches a mole or mouse in our yard or garden patches, he'll bring it to show to Uncle Miltie or me, so we can praise him for being such a wonderful hunter."

"But . . ."

"If he didn't do that, we might not be able to have all the

pretty flowers and those vegetables Uncle Miltie and I like to grow. We do praise him, and thank him, too."

"Oh."

He needed to think that over, so there wasn't much conversation as they started walking again. The only other person in the park right now was the elderly woman Gracie knew to be a resident in the old Fairweather mansion.

Augusta Lawson looked sad, as usual, taking her doctor-prescribed daily constitutional.

Gracie introduced Elmo to her and inquired after her health. Normally she'd have tried cheering her up, but with Elmo at her side the most she could hope was that the blessing of his presence would offer Augusta a taste of joy—of the sort only children can give.

Seeing her grandson yawn again, Gracie commented, "I think it's naptime for both of us."

He shook his head. "I'm not sleepy, Gramma—not one little bit!"

She gave a large yawn herself. "Well, I'm getting a little tired, so I'd just as soon head for home. We don't have to sleep, but maybe you could pick one or two books, and we could read them."

"Okay. That sounds really nice."

They each drank a glass of milk when they got back to the house. Then, with her recliner fully stretched out, she read his two choices. Soon he was asleep in her arms.

"Want me to carry him up to bed?" Arlen asked when he came in a little later.

She shook her head. "I've hungered for this closeness for far too long, dear, and am in no hurry to give him up."

"I know." His smile was gentle as he looked at his son. "I could never have imagined how much I'd love this little guy. And his mother."

"Isn't love wonderful?" she asked. "We as humans too often underappreciate the blessings God gives us."

"I'm afraid we do. Even though I was raised in this family where love abounded, I always took it for granted. And then I got out in the world, where I see far too many who've never once experienced the kind of genuine love you and Dad had for one another and for me."

She blinked away moisture as she reached for his hand. "Thanks, dear, for one of the most wonderful things ever said to me."

"I should have said it before, because I've thought it many times." He leaned over to kiss her cheek, then drew in a deep breath and squared his shoulders. "I obviously still have a lot to learn."

Uncle Miltie came into the room in time to hear those last words. "Me, too."

And Gracie made it unanimous with, "So say we all!"

She could hardly believe it when she woke to see that the

clock hands stood at four o'clock. She considered getting up and doing something about preparations for the evening meal, and even shifted Elmo a bit, intending to transfer him to the seat as she wriggled out from beneath him. However, she relaxed again when her movements brought him to near-consciousness.

Arlen came in again a little later, talking fairly loudly with Uncle Miltie, but Gracie decided it was her own sibilant "*Hush!*" that caused Elmo to shift restlessly, then open his eyes wide.

He was immediately sitting up and telling his father about their adventures on the swings, which were almost, though not quite, like the ones back home in New York.

However, his major concern was, "Did Gooseberry come back?"

"He's out on the porch, curled up on a chair," Uncle Miltie reassured him. "Did he wander off for a time?"

"Yeah—over at the park. Gramma thought maybe he was hunting a bug."

"Could be. They have Most Wanted posters out on him in the bug towns around here."

"*Huh?* Bug towns? Do bugs have towns? And what's a 'Mos' wanted poster?' Gramma said Gooseberry sometimes *eats* bugs!"

"Well, I've never visited them, but I'm sure they're there, and the bugs' opinion is that Gooseberry's a bad criminal, since he stalks and kills them."

"*Ooo!*" Elmo squirmed out of the recliner and ran through the kitchen and outside, checking out Gooseberry's present behavior. He looked innocent enough, there on the cushioned wicker chair. Licking his paw, he regarded little Elmo through his whiskers.

Gracie now got up, as well. "Dinner will be a little later than anticipated," she informed them. "I'd expected to get the meat on earlier, but taking a nap with my grandson took priority."

"No surprise there," Uncle Miltie said. "I'd probably starve if he never went back to New York. Hear that, Arlen?"

Marge dropped by in time to be invited to share the supper Gracie had prepared.

Uncle Miltie teased her about eating twice at every meal— once at her house and once at theirs. But she was unrepentant. "You know me—never wanting to hurt Gracie's feelings!"

"*Hmmph!*" This was accompanied by a look at Arlen. "She thinks she gets away with excuses like that!"

Arlen glanced toward his mother. "Are you going to call a time-out, or should I?"

"The only thing to do is ignore them both."

"As for her," Uncle Miltie used his fork to point at Marge, "when she stops talking all the time we'll have to hold a mirror to her mouth to see if she's still breathing."

"At least I leave the corn where it belongs—in cans!"

Gracie felt compelled to say, even as she laughed, "Hey, you two! My grandson's here, and we don't need to set such a horrible example!"

Finally, Arlen had the inspiration to propose a Scrabble game, saying it would be better to have a real match of wits rather than an exchange of insults.

That was approved by all of the adults, and Elmo was given the building-block set that had long ago been his father's. It was something he always demanded—politely, of course—when he arrived for a visit at his grandmother's house.

Arlen's *beguine* was challenged, then accepted after it proved to be the right spelling for a real dance. There was more of an argument about Uncle Miltie's *dozuki*. Although it didn't show up in their dictionary, he insisted it was a Japanese tool to make dovetails, "I saw that in one of my woodworking magazines just last week." He went into the living room, found the article, and brought it out to read aloud. Still, the others were unconvinced of its legitimacy.

There was grumbling about foreign words until the older man retorted, "So's *pastrami*, and I didn't challenge you on that, woman!"

Marge sighed. "Let's let him get away with it this time, or we'll never finish!"

It was over a half-hour later when Arlen added his last square, an *E*, to the end of *AFFAIR* across—which also was used as the last letter of the up-and-down "DONE."

"Gosh," he looked around as though sincerely meaning it when he said, "it's awfully hospitable of the three of you to let me win!"

Marge pushed back from the table and got to her feet. "That's what we are—hospitable!"

Uncle Miltie nodded. "In her case, it means ready to be committed to one. Let's just hope they throw away the key!"

Marge looked as if she was about to say something, then thought better of it. "Bye, guys!" she called as she headed out the back door.

"Bye, Marge!" Gracie replied, echoed by her menfolk.

It was a soft "Mom?" that now got Gracie's full attention.

"What is it, dear?"

"You have some particular suspicions, don't you?"

She came to sit beside him. "Suspicions, yes. Facts, no."

"What do you really think's going on?"

"I wish I knew."

His eyes looked directly into hers. "Mom. . . ?"

Her gaze dropped to her hands, and she was surprised to see that the right one was tightly gripping the edge of the tabletop. She forced herself to make it lie quietly in her lap, but was almost sure her son understood the strain she felt.

"It could be anyone."

"But which of the 'anyones' do you consider most likely?"

"I'm not . . . sure."

He offered a small smile of encouragement. "Come on, pick one, Mom—anyone."

"Well, Tom ran against Elmo one time and I don't believe he had the slightest doubt that he'd win—but he didn't."

"And...?"

"Well, he'd done some not very nice politicking along the way, and I think he was sort of afraid Elmo would make him pay for that. After all, Tom has a law degree, and I've heard—though I don't know this as a fact, so I'm no better than all those other rumormongers I'm so steamed about—that he and his wife once had planned to use Willow Bend and its mayor's job as a stepping stone for state office."

"What kind of 'not very nice politicking' did he engage in?"

"For quite a while there, Tom had a camera with him wherever he went, even to the town's big anniversary bash that your father was so excited about near the end of his first term. There was at the time a great deal of nostalgia for what was called an old fashioned hoedown.

"Elmo went along with this, and a group largely made up of seniors practiced for weeks with their fiddles and guitars, and they brought in someone to call the dances."

He grinned at her. "I don't remember ever seeing or hearing of you and Dad square-dancing."

Her answering smile was one of almost embarrassment. "That's because I'd never done it—somehow, nobody I ever dated cared for it, so I hadn't learned. And your Dad had never tried it either but, being mayor, felt he should at least attempt it.

"So, some of the guys and their wives said they were going to see to it that 'Mr. and Mrs. Willow Bend'—that's what they called us, just friendly teasing—wouldn't shame our fair town. We were invited to one of the senior citizens' practice affairs, where they had a couple of fiddlers and a caller."

She paused and he leaned closer. "Was it fun learning?"

She sighed, remembering that evening—and the next week. "That evening was fun. Neither of us would have taken home any prizes, that's for sure, but it was so fast, so energetic, that by the time the first square—or whatever it's called—was over, I was laughing so hard and was so breathless that I just dropped into a chair.

"Somebody brought me a soda and everyone was laughing and encouraging us to try again, which we did."

"Sounds like a wonderful evening."

"It was—and so was the First Annual Willow Bend Anniversary Hoedown."

"But. . . ," Arlen was trying to figure out where this was leading, "then why don't you look and sound happier in recounting these events?"

"Because, only a day or two later pictures started showing up all over town. Of me, swirling or twirling so much that my skirt was flipped way up, and I was looking up at some of my men partners with pure joy. And your dad was shown with his hand a bit above or below the waistband of the fancy garments of some of the women in our square—and laughing with delight!"

"I'd love to see those photos."

"You don't understand, Arlen! They were enlarged, and mounted on posterboard—with big black words saying— BEHOLD YOUR MAYOR AND HIS FEMALE—*female*, not *wife*, I'll have you know—and FREE WILLOW BEND OF THIS BAWDY COUPLE! and RETURN DIGNITY TO THE OFFICE.

He stared at her. "Certainly nobody took those seriously! It sounds ludicrous!"

"Well, *I* did!"

"What about Dad? He didn't, did he?"

She sank back into her chair. "He didn't seem to—but he wouldn't have let on if he did."

He sat there staring at her and she couldn't keep from squirming. "I'm sorry if I've disappointed you, but you did ask. . . . I understand that maybe you had to have been there at the time."

He gave her a slow smile and reached for her hand. "You could never disappoint me, Mom. It's just that I suddenly realized that, with you always being there helping smooth things for everyone else, I never even suspected how vulnerable you might be."

"I—shouldn't have mentioned this." It's an ugly little story, because something innocent was twisted."

He leaned across the corner of the table and put his arm around her. "I'll always be grateful for your sharing it. I imagine even Dad didn't realize how much this hurt you."

She looked at him steadily. "And, though you might not believe this, I didn't fully realize it either until right now, which is really weird."

She wasn't certain where the conversation was heading, but was surprised again when Arlen asked, "Did you see Tom taking those pictures?"

She shook her head. "I was having such a good time that I don't remember anyone taking pictures—except for Rocky's photographer, Ben Tomlinson, and his photos were in the *Gazette* the following day—very nice ones, by the way."

"Do you have any that I could see?"

"I believe I mailed you that copy of the *Gazette*, didn't I?"

He nodded. "But the other ones, those on the posterboards?"

"Well. . ." She'd had no intention of ever showing those to anyone, but why had she not destroyed them? Maybe she had anticipated this very moment.

"Please?"

She hesitated another moment or two before getting to her feet with a sigh, and moving slowly around the table to her little office. Pulling the boards out from behind her file cabinet, she carried them to the kitchen, pausing at the counter for a paper towel to wipe off the tops "just in case they're dusty from being there such a long time."

She watched his expression as he looked at one of the large pictures after another, then up into her eyes. He was smiling broadly. "You were quite a *female*, Mom."

Then, registering her gasp of dismay, he added, "And you still are—in the very best meaning of that perfectly good word.

"Just look at this one—your joy, your happiness is so effervescent, so exuberant that I'd challenge anyone other than a confirmed misanthrope to keep from smiling when looking at it!"

"But it was used as a put-down, used against my wonderful husband!"

"And I'd bet dollars to doughnuts, as Uncle Miltie would put it, that this particular smear campaign backfired. Didn't Dad win that election in a virtual landslide?"

"He wasn't running, but it didn't matter, dear. This was right before that next election time . . . right before the accident when your father was killed."

He squeezed her hand again, then brought it up to hold against his cheek. "I'm sorry, Mom—I wasn't thinking. I remember his choice and why he made it."

She neither brushed away nor apologized for the tears that had come, unbidden, into her eyes. "No reason to apologize, dear. Our memories play tricks on all of us, don't they? Like now, looking at these pictures again, I see the gray beginning to show in my then-brown hair. Yet now I think of myself— see myself—as an actual redhead.

"Perhaps I should let it go back to natural—which would probably by now be much more gray than in that photo."

"In case you're wondering, I couldn't care less about that," he said gently. "Your hair can remain as it is or be purple or chartreuse, if that would make you happy. You'll still be my Mom, the most wonderful mother in the entire universe!"

That brought a laugh. "Thanks, dear, but you won't have to lose sleep over those alternatives. This color," touching her hair with her fingertips, "was an outward symbol of my decision to live in the present, not the past. As of now, I wish to keep it, not because I need it for that purpose anymore, but because I, personally, like it."

"And I do, too. . . you look great to me."

"Thank you, my darling."

SUNDAY MORNING Gracie woke up, not knowing whether she was looking forward to it or dreading it. The party later in the day, that is. She'd set the alarm, just in case, but was wide awake before four o'clock and in the kitchen just a few minutes later.

She'd told the other choir members she would provide all of the rolls, so her first task was preparing the dough. While that was rising, she made several casseroles of scalloped pineapple, an old standby that always proved a hit at Willow Bend affairs. It was sweet enough to serve on the dessert table if more was needed there, yet equally suitable to go alongside the vegetables and side dishes.

Would the twins really be surprised? She hoped they would, but their husbands had been so amateurish and passive about any planning that it seemed likely something was going to go awry.

Arlen came downstairs and offered to help as she was beginning to make the three small balls of dough to put in each greased cup of several muffin pans for cloverleaf rolls. When pajama-clad Elmo arrived a little later and his father described to him the different fancy rolls he used to help his mother make when he was Elmo's age, the small boy begged to create some of those, also.

So, as Gracie worked away, her son and grandson made butterfly rolls, twists, knots, and salt sticks. "Bravo!" Gracie applauded little Elmo. "Your dad's a good teacher."

After so many hours of such dedicated baking, they barely made it to church on time. Gracie hurriedly put on her choir robe after arriving at the end of the once-more-through-the-anthem rehearsal Barb always insisted upon. Amy sang her solo part beautifully, as usual, and Gracie was tempted to remind Barb of her anxiety about Amy's hoarseness. But it was better not to, of course.

Nobody mentioned the twins' birthday, but Tyne murmured, "Today's our birthday!" as she stood in front of Gracie waiting for the first note of the processional hymn which would signal their entry into the sanctuary. Tyne giggled happily, looking over at her sister.

Gracie whispered, "I know. Happy birthday!" She always sent them cards—as she did to all her fellow choir members—but this time her birthday greetings would arrive in the mail the next day.

She was thrilled at Elmo's appearance up in front, a little later, when the children were all invited to come close for the weekly children's sermon, one of Gracie's favorite parts of the service. She listened closely as Pastor Paul welcomed the youngsters and asked, "Did any of you do anything to help someone recently?"

A number of hands shot up, including Elmo's. When his turn came, he said happily, "I helped Gramma and Dad make rolls this morning."

I just hope he doesn't say they're for a dinner here at the church, Gracie thought with a gulp.

But she needn't have worried for Pastor Paul merely said, "I'm sure she was very grateful for your help, Elmo," and went on to listen to what the next child had to contribute.

Then, the minister picked up from near the foot of the pulpit a rolled-up newspaper. "Is it always people for whom you do good things?"

One girl shook her head and stated, "I helped Daddy fill the bird feeder this morning, and I fed my puppy."

"Very good, Vanessa," Paul told her, and also commended several others. He unrolled the paper, but Gracie could see only that the final page consisted of colored pictures. "Do any of you see someone you know on this page?"

Elmo's finger touched the top picture as he stated, "That's my Gramma," and then he pointed toward the choir loft. "She's up there now."

Paul smiled. "Do you have any idea why her picture's in the paper?"

Gracie sank down just a little in her seat. What *was* she in for? The kitten had needed attention to its plight, not her. She'd noticed Rocky come in a few minutes earlier and, looking at him now, saw his broad, Cheshire Cat grin.

The pastor was pointing to one picture after another, showing how the kitten was unidentifiable in the first shots. "See? The poor little thing's so covered with burrs it could hardly move at all."

He reached carefully to the front of the pulpit, to a mound of actual burdock burrs, and gingerly pulled a few free from the rest. "Elmo's grandma—stand up, Gracie—and you stand up too, Les—found the kitty when it looked like this."

Some of the children got up from where they were sitting to look at the pictures more closely, not at all sure this was a cat. The young pastor continued, "Gracie Parks rescued this prickly little kitten, with the help of her own cat, Gooseberry, whom many of you know. Then Lester Twomley, another choir member, as it happens, appeared and drove them over to the office of Dr. Davena Wilkins.

"Do any of you know Dr. Wilkins?"

Several eagerly told of her taking care of their pets. "There she is, in this picture and there, and there, and that one," Vanessa stated.

He nodded, then showed them, "And in each of these, you

see more and more of the kitty, as the doctor and Mrs. Parks and Mr. Twomley pull the burrs off of her—which was difficult, since they are so very sharp, and they stick together."

"And here's what the kitten looks like now," he declared, pointing to the last snapshots. "Isn't she beautiful?"

Amidst the soft *oohs* and *ahs* of the children, Paul turned toward the door through which the choir had recently processed. "Would you please bring her in now, Doctor?"

And there was Davena Wilkins, wearing a thigh-length white labcoat over a brightly colored skirt and blouse, carrying the small black kitten. She was introduced to the children, then asked what had probably led up to her patient's predicament. In answer, she explained that many people who have kittens and puppies don't want to take them out to the country and leave them there.

"I don't believe most people intend to be cruel or mean when they do this," she told them, "but the fact is that baby animals have no idea how to catch food to eat, so many of them starve to death or they are caught and eaten by other animals. And they don't understand other dangers, either, like these awful burrs this kitten got into.

"She obviously tried real hard to get away from them, but more and more got on her, and they stuck together so tightly that when Gracie and Les brought her to me she could hardly move at all. And, as is shown in this picture, she could barely see anything.

"I even had to give her a shot because the pain from pulling off the burrs would have been too much for her to bear after what she'd already suffered." Several of the kids made a face at the word shot.

It was obvious that the veterinarian was interacting so well with these children and putting her message across so clearly that it was unlikely any of them would ever deliberately mistreat one of God's creatures. She obviously felt that this brief but poignant tale was important for the adults to hear and that it would have echoes in their lives, too. Gracie agreed with her.

Les leaned forward to whisper, "If only I had my camera now!"

Gracie turned enough to nod, but assumed he, also, had seen Ben Tomlinson up in the balcony. Ben was not a member here, but he was one of Rocky's photographers and that could only mean that the editor had been in on the planning of this, along with Paul and Davena.

The vet was now saying, in closing, that unless the owner claimed the kitten within the next several days, it would be put up for adoption.

Gracie heard a low, "*Uh-oh!*" from behind her and thought it was probably Marybeth Bower, Herb's wife, afraid her own twins would plead for ownership! She guessed other parents in the congregation were suddenly worrying about the same thing!

It was soon time for the anthem. It had only three verses, all sung in harmony, each of which was followed by the chorus, consisting of a simple, repeated, "And I shall raise" and "My voice in praise."

"And I shall raise

(And I shall raise)

My voice in praise

(My voice in praise)

And sing my love for Thee."

Thank goodness nobody had brought their casseroles with them to church, Gracie thought to herself. She'd given clear instructions but someone might have disregarded her, finding convenience of delivery more important.

A few of those in the congregation wished Tish and Tyne birthday blessings after the worship service and during Sunday School, but no big fuss was made of it.

"Daddy," Elmo began, as they walked out of the building, "can I take that kitty home with us?"

Arlen opened the car door and helped his son into the car seat, making sure he was securely fastened. "Oh, the owner will probably show up—or, for that matter, somebody else may have already asked for her."

"But if not, Daddy," the little boy's voice was filled with a joyful determination, "then can I have her?" His eyes sparkled at the thought.

"We'll see." Arlen's tone was kind but dismissive.

Gracie was listening, knowing all too well what a familiar rite of passage this was. Who would prevail? Her money was on little Elmo.

"But Daddy, we have to ask right away, before someone else does."

His father was getting into the front seat and fastening his own seatbelt. "This is an Indiana cat, Elmo. She might not like living in New York."

Gracie tried to hide her smile, quite sure that argument wasn't going to work—and it didn't, of course. Her grandson pleaded, "I won't tell her she's in New York, Daddy, and she prob'bly won't even know."

Uncle Miltie started coughing, up there in the front seat, and Arlen looked at him with raised brows. "Quite a cough you have there, Uncle Miltie."

It took a second or two to catch his breath before the older man agreed, "It does seem that way, doesn't it?"

Elmo asked, "Do we have a vet'narian in New York?"

Arlen established eye contact with his son in the rearview mirror. "There have to be lots of them there, Elmo, though I don't know any personally."

"We can find one, can't we?"

Arlen's gaze had shifted from the mirror to the other cars around. "No matter where people live, there are always doctors for people, and for dogs and cats."

The child gave a huge sigh that must have totally emptied his lungs. "Good! Then we don't have to worry, do we?"

Uncle Miltie's condition must have been contagious, for Gracie, also, coughed several times.

Even before she started getting a light lunch ready ("And it's going to be really light, you realize, since we're eating again in only three hours!") Gracie spread out on the kitchen table that morning's edition of their local paper, and the men joined her. "Les did a great job," her son stated.

"He certainly did—and with a totally new camera, at that."

She nodded. "It was such a gorgeous day, and we were just meandering along, and then Gooseberry found her."

"And," Arlen put his arm around her, "this is the point at which you would have given me a little mini-sermon when I was Elmo's age, isn't it? About God having you there at the right time and having that inquisitive cat of yours point out the kitten to you and give you the chance to save it?"

Uncle Miltie put in, "She still does that to me."

She ignored that last comment in order to respond to the one preceding it. "Well, it apparently worked. I'm delighted by the reassurance that you recognize the Lord's hand in everyday situations."

Arlen laughed. "As though this," indicating the first pictures of the nearly invisible kitten, "happens to most people—or cats—every day!"

"But equally important things are happening out there all the time, though we too often think of them as annoyances, problems, or insurmountable obstacles."

"You're right, Mom—and as you notice I am getting my mini-sermon after all."

It was her turn to laugh. "Well, you must admit you asked for it!"

"I did, didn't I? And I'd probably have been disappointed if you hadn't followed through."

After their lunch—comprised of a salad and bread-and-butter sandwiches—Uncle Miltie took Elmo onto his lap and read to him. They were both already napping in his comfortable recliner when Arlen asked, "Mom, have you ever gone through all of Dad's papers and records?"

She shook her head. "I couldn't at first—I was hurting too much—and then later, it somehow just didn't seem all that necessary."

"I can understand that, but when you talked to me on the phone about the rumors, the gossip, I got to wondering if there just might be something there—something that perhaps took place during those last weeks or months of Dad's life that might give some clue to understanding what's happening now.

"As I recall, he used to keep a journal. Did he continue that?"

She nodded. "But it was a private one—and I always honored that privacy."

"And I honor your integrity, Mom, I really do. But my dad—your husband—has been gone for a number of years now. Isn't it conceivable that his reputation is now being assailed because of something mentioned in his journals?"

"Of course—but I'm not sure I want to see what's there. Not only would I feel as though I'm betraying a trust but, should there be negatives about friends and neighbors—or me, for that matter—I'm still not ready."

"There won't be negatives about you, Mom. He adored you and you know it!"

"Yes, I do, and will be eternally grateful for that. But you do understand, dear, that we were both fully human, and that means strong-willed. So we did occasionally have some fairly intense discussions and arguments."

He laughed. "I remember a few of those—but I never, ever worried about the depth and stability of your love for one another and of your marriage and our family."

"I never before admitted to myself," she said thoughtfully, "that what I feared I couldn't handle was if he should have written a journal entry at one of those blessedly few times when we weren't quite as close as usual."

She'd been focusing her gaze on her hands, clasped there on the table, but now looked up into the eyes of her son, so much like those of his father. Smiling, she pushed herself up to her feet. "But yes, dear, you do have a point—one Jesus referred to very long ago, about perfect love casting out all fears."

She led the way to her office—which used to be Elmo's. Many of his books had been given to Arlen and some had been relegated to boxes under the eaves, but the majority remained on the shelves—including years and years of journals. She took down the final two. "Here, darling, you take this one."

He looked at her with admiration. "You really are something."

"I'll look through this one," Gracie said, smiling at him.

He thumbed the pages. "I'm—not sure what to be looking for, are you?"

"Not really, but I'll be at least pausing to scan anything about anyone who by the furthest stretch of my imagination might have been angry at Dad—or he at them."

He nodded. "Okay, but I'll probably have to keep bugging you about things—like here, when he says Hammie called him about some 'rather pressing problem.' How can we possibly know what the outcome was?"

"I—suppose we just keep on reading. If nothing further's said on the subject, we'll have to assume everything turned out okay."

There were, she soon saw, numerous one-time references to

individuals. She knew almost all of them, but when it came to their problems, there were ones she'd never have guessed at and others about which she hadn't had a clue. And Elmo had not made an unusual amount of entries during his last month on earth.

She was halfway through her journal when Arlen asked, "What do you know of Syd Browning?"

She briefly explained about his having been fired as police chief but that she'd never known why. Her son then read aloud the brief statement: "'*Rocky tells me Syd's been trying for a law enforcement job in Missouri. Think he's taking care of that.*'"

He looked at her quizzically. "Know what this is about?"

"What I do know is that the conditions under which Syd was allowed to resign specified that he couldn't go into police work again. So, yes, I can imagine Rocky's getting word to those needing that information."

Arlen put a paper clip on that page and went on scanning. Gracie also used these on pages where Tony or Harvey were mentioned. And there was one more that she unhesitatingly flagged in this way—Willow Bend's present mayor, Thomas Ritter.

She'd come to the end. "If there are specific clues here, Arlen, I've failed to find them."

"Me, either," he admitted. "But I worry that I missed something. My sixth sense tells me I have."

"Me, too." But then she held out her book toward him. "How about trading?"

They each read on, but nothing set off any major alarm for either of them. It had been a good idea, but they had made no progress.

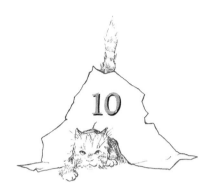

O H, MY GOODNESS!" Gracie jumped to her feet after glancing at her watch. "I was so involved with these journals that the time got away from me! I was supposed to be at the church by now!"

"At least we'd loaded the car before starting our research, so you can buzz straight on over. If our sleeping handsomes don't wake up on their own within a half hour, I'll help them out. I'd like us to be there in time to be useful for at least a while before Tish and Tyne arrive."

Her responding smile was as much for his play on the *sleeping beauties* term as for his thoughtfulness.

"Great! See you there!" she called as she hurried out.

Marge, Marybeth, Barb and Rick Harding were already in the kitchen when she rushed inside, carrying the first two casseroles of scalloped pineapple. Marge told her, "We were about ready to send the rescue squad! You're always the first one here."

Gracie set her load on the counter. "I don't usually have my son and grandson with me." It was enough of an explanation, and an apology was hardly necessary, even if Marge's statement was true. She'd worked with these women so often that each knew her responsibilities and did them well—while also being ready to give someone else a hand.

The last of the table settings were being laid when Uncle Miltie arrived, scolding them for not waiting until he got there. "I'm the chief silverware man around here, and everyone knows it. Long John Silverware, that's me, shiver me timbers!"

"Well, you can put ice in the glasses, then fill them with water," Gracie suggested. "That's the closest to shivering I can think of."

He responded cheerfully, "Okay-dokey, I'll take care of that—in fact, I'm going to start right away on these ice-capades."

"Me, too," Elmo chimed in. "I can put the ice-capades in the glasses for you, Uncle Miltie, then all you have to do is pour in water."

"Good idea, little fellow," he approved. "It's great to have a partner when doing important jobs like this."

Gracie had bought bags of ice, so the idea was for Elmo to carefully lift cubes with tongs one at a time from the stainless steel bowl into which some had been poured.

However, he tired of this task by the time he got to the third table. Encouraged by his dad, he went to play outside with the other kids. Uncle Miltie heaved a sigh of relief as he took a plateful of ice cubes to the kitchen. Dumping these into one of the sinks, he said, "Elmo was willing, for sure, but had he 'helped' any longer, we'd have had to send out for more ice."

Gracie laughed. "At least you were getting your exercise, stooping over to pick them up as fast as he dropped them."

"Perhaps there's such a thing as child-sized tongs, but these don't fit that bill!" Brandishing them, he headed back to the tables.

Busy with many other things, Gracie didn't watch to see how he was coming along. It was some time later when she noticed that the job must be completed, for Uncle Miltie was nowhere to be seen. What's he up to now? she wondered. She also didn't realize that Arlen wasn't helping out any longer until she saw him coming down the hall with Pastor Paul, deep in conversation.

"Everything seems right on schedule," Marge declared, appearing at Gracie's shoulder.

"We know how to get the job done, don't we?"

"Well, even given the cluenessness of John and Bill, this is going to be a lovely party. The great thing is how you were able just to go with the flow, Gracie, and find the formula that would suit the event."

"We can thank my Elmo for that." Gracie smiled at her best friend. "When we first got married, I tried so very hard to do everything just right, to be perfect for the man I loved so much. That goal met with defeat the very first weekend following our honeymoon, when I totally forgot a buffet supper here at the church!

"I was devastated, sure I was the worst bride ever, but he insisted we come anyway—so we arrived with a bag of potato chips bought on our way! I'd have preferred staying home under the circumstances, but Elmo said, 'People want to get to know you, the only woman in the world with whom I'd choose to spend the rest of my life.

"'If you love me as I love you, you will hold your head high, admit that you're human enough to have forgotten one little thing, go on with life—and enjoy the evening.'

"I needed that lesson, both as it pertained to me and as it illuminated others. I still sometimes do stupid or confused things, but that makes me even more ready to give others a break, or the benefit of the doubt. And prayer does help."

"Sure does!"

"Since we're here in the church again for fellowship and eating together, I must say I've thought a great deal about one of the Parks Family Rules—'A dash of prayer helps any recipe.'"

"What would we do without that ingredient?"

"I don't want to ever find out!"

Gracie had wondered how the husbands were going to pull off the surprise part of the birthday party—but both insisted that their wives had no clue until Bill pulled into the church parking lot, saying, "I hope you don't mind our stopping at the church a minute before heading over to La Bella Cucina."

Tyne and Tish were still wearing what they had on for church, pretty dresses the exact color of their blue eyes, a little more flouncy or "feminine" than Gracie would have bought, but exactly right for them. They seemed thoroughly delighted at their surprise, greeting everyone and offering as many birthday hugs as they received.

Tish was the first to come into the kitchen to embrace her fellow choir members who'd helped. "Thanks so very, very much, every one of you! We never had . . ."

". . . any idea of what was being planned!" Tyne, following her, completed her thought, as happened so often in their very close, very loving sistership.

Everyone stood while Pastor Paul led in the prayer of thanksgiving for the abundance of food. He offered thanks, too, for the hands that had prepared the meal, and everyone who had helped, and especially for these sisters whose birthday was being celebrated. Wasn't it glorious how they were loved by their families, their church and their community?

The guests filled their plates by going down either side of the loaded buffet tables. And before long the contents of many of the serving dishes were depleted and being replaced. But, still, a large quantity of food was left when everyone was seated and had begun eating.

Now came those speeches and teasing remarks which almost always accompany birthdays of dear friends and relatives. Yet as Gracie looked out over the room, she was struck by the fact that there were guests present she wouldn't ever have expected to see.

For example, Tony Randolph was sitting at a table off to the side. As far as she could tell, he'd come alone—at least he was doing a little talking, and then mostly when someone first spoke to him.

Meanwhile, Mayor Tom Ritter was sitting with his wife Sherry about three tables away, and seemed to be doing most of the talking at his end. Nearby, Jessica Larson was loudly complaining about problems on the school board. But one of her tablemates finally succeeded in getting the conversation onto a different track by commenting what a great band the high school had had this year and how it had won statewide awards in the spring.

Harvey Smith, also apparently alone, had little to say, though his gaze appeared to miss nothing.

Dear Lord, Gracie prayed silently, *if there's something I should be seeing or hearing, please help me fathom it. Don't let me concentrate on the wrong person to such an extent that I'll miss whatever's more important.*

Tish and Tyne were going together from table to table, thanking people for making this such a wonderful day for them. Only when the clean-up got underway did Gracie get an earful from Uncle Miltie. "I don't know, Gracie, what I've done so awful in life that I had to get stuck at the table with our mayor and his wife!"

"It was really that bad? I didn't notice you there."

"Well, Missus mayor was indignant there was no head table for Tish and Tyne and *them*. After all, her husband's far too busy to come to just anyone's birthday party and then only be part of the cast of thousands."

"She said that?"

"Those might not have been her exact words, but her meaning was not only clear but loud."

Lord, give me strength....

"Well, judging from your reaction, it's a good thing the twins were spared. And it's their day, after all."

He looked at her and nodded, "You're right, of course."

When inviting their guests, Bill and John had said to not bring presents—just come and help celebrate. However, many brightly wrapped gifts were on and under a large table in the corner. So, as the kitchen crew took care of their responsibilities and the men folded the other tables and carried them back to the storage area, the remaining guests moved near enough to see what had been brought.

Gracie observed some of these as they were *ooh'ed* and *ah'ed* over—and was grateful she herself didn't have to find places in her home for all these tokens of love which, for the most part, were things she'd have no use for!

Her hands were in the very warm dishwater when she came to the decision she'd probably begun checking those journals at too late a period. Therefore, when Herb stopped on his way out to tell her and the others what a great job they'd done again today, she wasted no time before asking him, "How long have you been here in Willow Bend?"

"Think I'm overstaying my welcome?" he teased.

"Hardly! But answer my question, please. I feel so vague and forgetful about dates, and I'd like to know this one."

"Well," he said, "these six years have flown by, and Marybeth and I have been happy here."

She needed a more exact date. "You came in the summer, didn't you?"

"*Um-hmmm.* It was July 19 when we officially moved, but I'd been staying at Cordelia's since mid-June."

"And do you by any chance know how long your predecessor had been gone?"

"I always like to think of my predecessor as being your husband. As you recall, he'd filled in for that nine-week interval after Syd left."

She glanced around to make sure nobody was listening to their conversation, and found that most people, including Marge and those who'd been washing and drying dishes, were now watching the gift opening. "I remember that all too well! However, may I ask a question? Do you know exactly why Syd left?"

He hesitated. "I . . . found out some things for sure . . . and suspect a lot more."

"That's how it is for me, as well." She realized he was not offering to give information and that she had no right to ask. "Elmo never shared anything like that with me, but I'm almost positive Syd was forced to hand in his so-called resignation."

She was now sure she'd been right. Herb gave no sign he'd even heard her comment, just said he was going to stop at the office for a few minutes on his way home. "The kids are playing over at our neighbor's, so I'm going to tell Marybeth I'll soon be picking them up and fix sandwiches or something. That way she won't feel she has to rush home."

"Your little ones are blessed by having such caring, loving parents."

"Hey, in my profession I've seen far too many products of parents who just don't care."

Gracie, too, left earlier than most. "I've boxed up nine meals for some of our shut-ins and elderly parishioners," she'd explained to Marge and Eleanor. "I'm dropping them off on my way home."

She did not stay at any of the homes to chat, however, for she was eager to get home. After all, her son and grandson would be leaving the following day.

She wanted to spend all the time she could with them.

She told Arlen about the insight she'd had while washing dishes. Maybe they'd had the time frame wrong, she suggested and immediately he proposed, "Then let's go over another one or two of those journals."

"Do we want to spend our last evening here together doing that?"

"I'd sure like some answers, Mom, if at all possible."

She nodded. "So would I."

It was in the third of these journals that they came across cryptic references to "SB," which by context they figured had to be Sydney Browning.

"Here's another," Arlen said, turning a page. "'SB's sporting a new Jeep—Interesting, isn't it? Any connection with HS?'"

They looked at one another thoughtfully and she said, "A Jeep and an 'HS'—that's got to be Harvey Smith, since his dealership handles those, as well as other makes."

"What kind of reputation does he have—a good one, as far as you know?"

"I can't say for sure. I, personally, don't know him well, but do recall your dad's once saying that, though he'd love to sometime have a Jeep, he'd never get it from Harvey."

"Anything more you remember about that—or about him?"

She shook her head. "Nothing specific, just little things. I never paid too much attention, since our paths seldom crossed."

She went back one more volume then, since anything leading up to hanky-panky would perhaps have taken place earlier. Those initials were mentioned there about six weeks previously, *"HS to see me in mayoral capacity this morning—about 'fixing' a ticket. Told him nothing doing—I'd never expunge drunken driving from an accident report, especially this one."*

A few pages later there was an addendum, *"Saw HS in town today. He carefully avoided 'seeing' me."* And about ten pages after that was the brief, *"Gave H and M notice as to watching at all times. Think they'll not take many more chances."*

Arlen mentioned some time later, "Isn't it odd there's no reference to your present mayor?"

"The Ritters came on the scene a bit later than this," said Gracie, indicating the volumes they were now perusing. "Although his official bio includes a law background, he apparently took early retirement from some managerial department in an automotive company or something. His wife Sherry explains that they were looking for the quality of life only a small town could offer."

He laughed. "That's got to be a direct quote, right?"

"I'm afraid you're right—but I can't laugh since, having bought and completely modernized one of the oldest houses in the area, they're now dead set on trying to change many of the very things they originally seemed to find so desirable about Willow Bend."

"Yet you're pushing for the veterinarian to run for mayor." His eyebrows arched in question. "Isn't she more or less a newcomer, too?"

"But she's totally different! Dave—Davena—is warm and comfortable with everyone, and makes them feel that way. You saw her in church this morning—and she's just as real and natural at town-council meetings. She does speak up about things for the betterment of the community—but somehow she always makes sense and ruffles only the feathers that deserve it."

"Does that mean Tom Ritter's?"

Gracie grinned at her son. "My opinion of Tom Ritter, and yours, is shared by Dr. Wilkins is all I can say."

"Which, I gather, doesn't cause you to lose sleep at night."

"At meetings you can actually see the man bristle when your dad's name comes up as various subjects are under discussion." She sighed. "I doubt he'll be reelected—but I didn't expect him to make it the first time, so what do I know?"

They were still flipping pages, and found several more items that piqued their interest, but gave no answers.

Among these was, *"Tony came with HS today. Odd combination! Told them I couldn't help in this."* What especially interested them was the slanted line drawn through the "c" and the "w" placed above it, making the word, *wouldn't*.

Elmo went to bed early, and when Gracie came back downstairs after reading to him and tucking him in for the night, both Rocky and Marge were in the kitchen with Uncle Miltie and Arlen.

The Scrabble board was all set and ready, and Marge greeted her with, "It's about time you came, Gracie! We were almost ready to start without you."

"It's no contest—being with my perfect grandson is all I ask tonight."

Arlen now asked, "Is this the only game you guys ever play?"

"Oh, no, but it's our favorite," Marge told him. "One of the good things with this is that any number can play—you don't need an even number, like four for bridge."

"And nobody can get mad at anyone for not playing this card or that, since it doesn't require partners," Uncle Miltie pointed out.

"And it keeps us on our toes learning new words and how to spell them," Gracie put in.

"Like that stupid Japanese tool you used last time, Uncle Miltie!"

"It's not stupid, Marge, if it works—whether in regard to making keyholes or getting letters onto the board!" he protested righteously.

Gracie sat there shaking her head for a moment before putting down two of her own squares—and making twenty-one points! Arlen looked at her and grinned. "Way to go, Mom! Show 'em how to do it!"

"We don't encourage cheerleading," Uncle Miltie told him.

"Right, but I'm not planning to take this too seriously, 'cause I'm just here occasionally. It's the rest of you I'm concerned about."

Gracie suspected his mind wasn't totally given to the game tonight, and she, too, was thinking about those journal-entries. *I'll definitely go through them page-by-page—as I should have long ago. I have no business, dear Lord, asking You to dump answers in my lap if I'm not willing to do my homework!*

Marge was the first to leave, and after Uncle Miltie went in to watch the late news the other three continued sitting at the table. "Rocky, I have to ask something," she finally said. "There's an entry in Elmo's journal about *you* taking care of it when Syd was found to be applying for a position as police chief somewhere."

There was a faint flicker of his eyelids, but the editor's voice was calm. "*Hmmm*, I wonder what he meant by that."

"No, you don't, Mr. Rocco Gravino! You know perfectly well what that's about!"

His glance went to her son, then back to her. "There may be some things he didn't want others to know about—not for his own sake, but others'."

"It had something to do with a gold-colored Jeep?"

He pushed back from the table and got to his feet. "I don't know everything that happened, but your husband was very upset."

"It wasn't like him to deliberately let evil triumph."

"He didn't have proof, and the only way he could possibly get that would be to make such a stink that everyone in Indiana, if not the whole country, would know of it. And they were extremely clever. When, as Mayor-*and*-Chief-of-Police, Elmo checked the official records, stuff was already conveniently missing from the files."

Arlen was sitting there perfectly still, except for his eyes, which watched the others as his mother now asked, "It was . . . about Benny, wasn't it?"

Rocky started for the door. "Good night, Gracie—and have a safe trip tomorrow, Arlen."

She took a huge leap into something she'd not previously considered, "Was it Harvey Smith—or was it Martin, his son?"

"Gracie! Please!"

"Rocky, what do you know?" She cast a pleading look in his direction.

"We tried—but there was nothing provable. Not ever."

He paused just before going out of the door. "In case you didn't know, Martin, Harvey's only son, died two years ago down in Tallahassee, from a drug overdose."

"Oh."

With one foot already on the porch, Rocky bent back inside to add, "And Benny's mom, his only close relative, died last fall."

She heard his footsteps as he crossed the porch and went down the steps. Arlen came to her, and held his mother as she cried.

ARLEN CAME BACK from putting luggage in his car as Gracie was pouring batter onto the waffle iron. "Have you seen your grandson recently?"

"He was here a few minutes ago, asking where Gooseberry was. I said I thought he was on the porch."

"Well, neither of them's here now." He looked at the already poured milk and orange juice, then at what she was doing. "I'd better call him in."

"*Um-hmmm*, the first of these will be ready by the time his hands are washed."

But the child had not come by the time the second of the waffles was baked. Nor the third.

"Boys!" Uncle Miltie said, as though that one word explained everything. "It's so easy for them to do their disappearing acts right when you want them." He took his usual place at the table. "Come on," he invited. "We might as well eat these while they're hot."

Gracie, however, removed the last waffle from the iron and pulled the cord from the wall socket. "Go ahead, Uncle Miltie. I'll be back in a minute. Elmo's such a friendly little guy, he's probably gone into one of the neighbor's houses and doesn't hear his dad calling."

Uncle Miltie and Arlen followed her outside. "Gooseberry's not here, either," he told his great-nephew. "Come morning, that cat's usually begging for your mom to go with him for a walk."

"I hope Elmo didn't succumb to his pleading!"

"Is he still bugging you to adopt the kitten?"

"It's good we're leaving this morning!" Arlen grimaced. "He never gives up when there's something he really wants."

"Sounds like a normal kid then, doesn't he?" Uncle Miltie chuckled. "Quite a bit of his old man in him, I'd say. Remember when you came to visit your aunt and me when you were about this age? I made the mistake of taking you to play miniature golf the very first night you were there, and you coaxed and begged to go back every evening after that!"

Arlen laughed. "I do remember. Things seem pretty important when your whole world is so small!" He started walking toward his mother, who was emerging from the third house down the street.

"No sign of him yet," she told him, then called across the

street to an elderly man on his knees by the bed of roses. "Did you by any chance see my little grandson this morning?"

"What?" His head tilted, right ear turned more directly toward her as he leaned back on his heels. "What did you say, Gracie?"

She started across. "My grandson was playing outside while waiting for breakfast. He's a little guy, about this tall, and...."

His face wrinkled even more with his smile. "Ah, yes—a fine little man-child. Elmo, he said his name was, like his granddaddy."

She nodded. "Do you know where he might be?"

"He said he was taking Gooseberry for a walk." He pointed down the street. "They went that way, not very long ago."

"Thanks for the help." Turning, she said, "I'm going to check at the park; he enjoyed that the other day, so he may have returned."

Her son started in her direction. "I'm coming with you."

She hesitated, then headed back toward the house. "It might be best for you and Uncle Miltie to stay around here. I'll take my cell phone, so you can reach me if he and Gooseberry just went around the block or something."

"I'll get it for you, Mom." He bounded up the steps, and was back in a few seconds. "You can call us if the little rascal's over there enjoying the swings. In the meantime, Uncle Miltie'll watch over things here while I walk around the block this way," he said, indicating the opposite direction from the one pointed to by her neighbor.

Gracie disciplined herself not to seem excessively worried. As she found herself passing Harvey Smith's car dealership, she did not wave or call a greeting, and was relieved at his giving no sign of seeing her, though she was sure he had.

Right now her only concern was little Elmo.

She arrived at the park, and entered, experiencing a deeper disappointment than she could have anticipated. She'd been so sure this was where he'd be!

Augusta Lawson was walking toward her on one of the diagonal paths; she seemed to be going a bit faster than usual—and was actually smiling! Gracie walked toward the elderly woman, about to ask if she'd seen Elmo, but Augusta beat her to the punch with, "You do have the dearest little grandson, Gracie!"

"You saw Elmo this morning?"

"I did, just a little while ago. He and your cat were here in the park. He was trying to make the swing go higher. I went over and pushed him for a little while and we got to talking."

"About. . . ?"

"He said he needed to go to the animal clinic, but couldn't remember just where it was. I told him I'd walk over with him, but he said he had to hurry real fast, because he and his daddy were leaving soon for New York. He was sure he could run faster than I could walk.

"So I watched him cross the street, and told him very carefully how to get there."

Gracie was already turning away as Augusta added, "But then I got to wondering if you had any idea where he was, so I was glad to see you right now as I was starting for your house."

"Thanks very much!"

"I'm sure he's all right," she called after Gracie.

Oh, Lord, please take care of him. This is Willow Bend and not New York City, but still, he has to cross several streets. And though I'm sure Arlen and Wendy have given him training as to safety instructions, I'd sure appreciate Your watching out for him. And for Gooseberry, too.

She was almost running by the time she got to the end of the first block, but paused at that corner to check all three directions.

She crossed the street and was hurrying up the next block when her cell phone buzzed. "Hello?"

"Hi, Gracie, it's Herb. Your uncle just called the station to say you're out looking for Elmo. Want me to join in the search?"

"Thanks, Herb. I appreciate it, but someone just told me she thinks he's going to Davena's. I suspect he wanted to say 'Goodbye' to a little black kitten."

"You're heading there now?"

"I'm almost there."

She turned at the next corner and went another block. The animal clinic had been on the very edge of Willow Bend when Dr. Benfer opened it over a half-century earlier and, though a subdivision had been added since then, its freshly painted whiteness and green trim blended in with the rest of this residential area.

She walked across the parking area for All Creatures, opened the door, walked in—and was dismayed to find only two men there. "Hi, Gracie," the postmaster, Vince Monroe, said cheerfully from where he sat on a straight chair at the far side of the waiting room.

She returned his greeting and said hello to the other man as she headed for the window where Davena's white-clad assistant was asking, "Looking for someone, Gracie?"

"Is my grandson here?"

She nodded. "I was about to phone you, but got tied up first with an incoming call."

"Where is he?"

"In with the doctor." She grinned at Gracie. "It seems that he and Gooseberry came to pay their respects to a certain rescued kitten we're keeping here."

"Uh-oh!"

Annie couldn't help laughing. "You can go in there now. I'm sure they'll all be happy to see you."

"We-e-ell," she replied. "The main thing is that he's safe. Still, I'd like to see for myself."

Before she'd taken even a few steps, she heard the squeal of tires, a car door slamming, and rushing feet. The outside door opened and Arlen was asking, "Is he here, Mom?"

She nodded as she turned the knob to the examining room where they both went inside. Elmo was sitting on the high metal table, holding the kitten against his chest and asking eagerly, "Daddy, we can take her home, can't we?"

His father was speaking at the same time. "Elmo! You know you aren't allowed to run off like this!"

"I didn't run off, Daddy! I just came to see the kitty. She likes me, see?" The kitten stretched up to lick his cheek and rub against it. "Please, Daddy?"

Gracie reached down to pet Gooseberry, who was rubbing against her leg.

The veterinarian was standing there smiling at Arlen and his boy. Suddenly there was the sound of loud talking in the waiting room, and the door burst open to let in Herb, with Paul right behind him, demanding, "Are you okay, Elmo?"

Davena was failing in her effort to look professionally stern and remain formal, and the sparkle in her dark brown eyes belied the firmness of her words, "This is not a public meeting place."

Paul explained, "Uncle Miltie put it on the prayer chain that Elmo was lost, so I was rushing out to the church's parking lot when Herb stopped long enough to tell me that the boy might be here."

Davena smiled even more broadly as she glanced out the window and then headed for the door. She opened it in order to greet two more arrivals. "The lost is found, gentlemen."

"Great!" Rocky cried, even as his photographer was raising his camera to begin taking pictures.

She made no protest, just moved to the side.

Everyone was talking at once until Elmo, holding onto the kitten with one hand, tugged on his father's sleeve. "Daddy— *please*, Daddy, let's take the kitty back with us. I'll take good care of her, so that she won't mind that we live in New York!"

The others could not know this last was in response to Arlen's rather weak argument of the day before, and Gracie made no effort to explain. Arlen was saying, "We'll have to check with your mother...."

"Yeah, Daddy, let's call. I'm sure she'll say it's okay!"

Arlen was obviously not as positive of that as his son, but did take out his cell phone and punch in numbers. "Hi, Wendy.... No, nothing's wrong, but we're getting a slightly later start than planned...." And then he told about the kitten and its rescue by Gracie, and of Davena's role in the drama.

To the delight of everyone, except maybe Arlen, who was still adjusting to the notion that where two travelers had arrived, three were leaving, the newly named Blackie was to become a member of the Manhattan Parks family.

Davena even provided a carrier for her, although Elmo declared he intended to hold her in his lap all the way.

"I don't know how good a traveler Blackie may be," the vet told him. "If she gets too tired and needs a little time to herself, or if you take a nap, she can be put in here."

"I'm a big boy now," he insisted, drawing himself up as tall as possible. "I won't have to take a nap!"

Arlen, however, accepted the carrier with gratitude. "Thanks, Dave. Depending on how active our Blackie is, I suspect this may come in very handy. I haven't known many calm kittens."

More time was spent on further details of cat comfort, like a clean terrycloth towel to pad the carrier. Soon, however, the trio was pulling out of the parking lot, followed by the *Gazette* team and Herb.

On her way out with Paul, Gracie thanked the very patient men who'd been in the waiting room when she'd arrived, and also a woman who'd arrived in the interim with her elderly cat.

She knew that Annie had explained what had taken place, so she only added, "I apologize for the delay, but you've made my little grandson very happy—and helped give a homeless kitten a loving family!"

Uncle Miltie's intake of breath while reading the next morning's paper brought Gracie to look over his shoulder.

Splashed across the front page was the headline: VETERI-NARIAN DAVENA WILKINS ENTERS THE RACE.

There was a shot of her, Elmo, Arlen, Gracie and the kitten next to the article—along with a key to more pictures at the back of the section! Gracie and Uncle Miltie, of course, looked at the photo spread before returning to the article, which quoted the vet as saying she'd originally hesitated when asked to enter the mayoral race.

"However, seeing how spontaneously and generously the whole town—police, news media, religious institutions and friends—responded to what could have been a major missing-child emergency, I realized how special this town is," she was reported as saying. "I'd be honored to serve Willow Bend, my adopted town, in any way, including becoming its mayor, if the voters so choose."

There was even information as to how one could go about voting for her as a write-in candidate!

Uncle Miltie chuckled. "I'll bet Tom and Sherry are having fits!"

She laughed with him. "As are Harvey and Tony."

"Especially since those guys have been practically standing on their heads for publicity and here's Davena getting pretty regular coverage!"

Davena's entry onto the political scene was the main topic of conversation everywhere Gracie went that day. At the deli,

Abe sounded a warning note. "You know, Gracie, it wouldn't surprise me if whoever started that other gossip is probably getting ready to launch an offensive against Davena. There'll be another spate of rumor-mongering, just you wait and see."

"Have you heard anything yet?"

"No." He shook his head. "And I'm hoping I won't. She's a fine woman, as well as being an excellent professional and a first-rate citizen. I'd sure hate to see anyone try to mess with her reputation."

"Me, too."

Gracie hadn't spent much time at the park with Gooseberry that morning and was about to leave when Augusta walked up to her. "I'm breaking up my exercise routine since coming home from the hospital," she explained, "doing some in the morning and some in the afternoon."

She then mentioned being very pleased to learn from the paper that little Elmo had arrived at the animal clinic safely—and had been allowed to adopt the kitten Gracie had rescued.

"I'm glad that fine young doctor's going to run for mayor," she continued. "It's probably not kind to say, but I really didn't want to vote for any of the other candidates—including Harvey, even if he *is* my son-in-law."

Somehow Gracie had forgotten that. Augusta went on, "I—still haven't forgiven him for so spoiling his son, my only grandson—and letting him get away with so much. But I truly did love that boy, and don't think I'll ever get over losing him like that."

She impatiently brushed away the tears collecting in her pale blue eyes.

"Of course you love him." Gracie purposely changed the tense that from past to present, knowing how much she herself still loved and missed her Elmo after all these years. Augusta smiled at her gratefully through her tears.

On her way home, seeing Harvey alone in the car lot, she walked in to greet him with a casual "Hi."

"Hello, Gracie."

There was no smile nor holding out of his hand. But she was determined to stay polite. "How are things going?"

"Good."

"I assume you saw the write-up in the paper this morning?"

He nodded, but said nothing.

"I just stopped by to say I will definitely not be running for mayor."

She saw a very slight flicker of his eyelids, but he remained silent. She went on steadily, "I thought you might be interested in knowing that I'd never said I would."

More silence. "Therefore, Harvey, I'd appreciate your stopping all those rumors and innuendoes you've been spreading."

"What do you mean?"

"I'm about to make a promise to you," she stated. "Should you do anything like that to Davena, I will share with the authorities everything I've figured out about Benny's death."

"I've no idea what you're talking about!" He glared at her, his eyes widened.

"Here's what I believe—had your son gotten help at that time, Harvey, perhaps he'd still be alive today. And that fact must make you lie awake at night."

"Gracie, I think you'd better go now."

She stared at him, unflinching. "Just one thing more. Should anything happen to Davena or to me because of my speaking to you, the truth will come out—I am not alone in knowing it."

"You're threatening me?"

"I just thought you might like to know how things stand." She leaned over and picked up Gooseberry, who'd been looking up at her with what appeared to be grave concern. "Someone should have done something about the situation long before this . . ."

His words now came through clenched teeth. "I'll say it one more time. Go!"

She was determined to finish. "It's especially tragic that it was one of the gentlest, most unselfish people in our area whose life was snuffed out that night. No matter how it happened, it's on your conscience, and I don't think you want anything else there."

She was still uneasy about Harvey's threatening demeanor as she set Gooseberry down on the sidewalk and headed for home. In a moment, however, she changed direction and went on to the police station. As she entered, she was relieved to find Herb standing in the outer office, talking to Lucille Murphy.

He must have seen how upset she was, for he motioned to her instantly, "Come with me, Gracie."

In his office, she sank into the chair next to the desk. "Tell me about it," Herb urged her.

"I have a confession, Herb. I—may have been incredibly stupid a few minutes ago."

He said nothing as she told him about her conversation with Harvey. "I'm almost positive my suspicions are correct, Herb, and I think it was necessary to do this, but . . ."

He waited patiently for her to continue. Gooseberry was sitting on the floor, looking up at her and occasionally *meowing* softly. Finally Herb picked him up and set him on Gracie's lap. Her hand began stroking him, and he began to purr loudly as she continued her account. When she'd finished, Herb asked, "Are you afraid of him, Gracie?"

"I—don't think so, not much right now—not for myself. But I want you to know about Elmo's journals. I didn't mention them to Harvey, but if he ever knew about Elmo's making entries almost every day, he could possibly put two and two together."

"Would you like me to put them in the safe? You could take them out as you needed them."

She nodded. "And I'd also like you to photocopy a few of the pages for me—and for you and for Arlen."

"Makes perfect sense to me," Herb told her.

They sat a few minutes more in companionable silence.

12

GRACIE ALWAYS LOVED the beautiful autumn days. They passed all too swiftly. She and Gooseberry did not walk to the park again during this period, choosing instead to wander through other parts of town and out the country lanes.

Reading the paper each day, she and Uncle Miltie kept watch over the mayoral contest. Davena Wilkins had the edge in overall favorable coverage. But it was hard to know whether the voters of Willow Bend were going to go for the tried and true, or for the idea of a fresh start.

Election day finally arrived. Uncle Miltie was a poll worker at the first ward site, the public library, while Cordelia and Eleanor did this at the fire hall, which was where those in the second ward voted. They all eagerly told voters how to either use the stickers provided, or to write in Davena's name.

There was great rejoicing at Gracie's and around town when the results finally were tabulated: Davena Wilkins had received almost as many votes as had the other three together!

"Congratulations, Mom!" Arlen cheered, receiving the news by phone. "From what I've seen, I think she's an excellent choice!"

"Me, too! And I also think she'll work well with the council members." She went on, "There are one or two who are so used to getting their own way in everything that at first she'll have her hands full, but she'll make out fine."

"And, knowing you, you'll be doing a lot of praying for her."

"Of course!" She laughed. "Hey, I'm still praying for you each day, so why not for her?"

"Why not indeed?" His voice sounded very serious at this point. "Thanks again for all those prayers, Mom. I'm always going to need them."

It was shortly after that when Rocky told her about Harvey Smith's having sold his dealership to a man from Cleveland, who'd be officially taking it over in a matter of weeks. Nothing was mentioned concerning Harvey's future plans, but Uncle Miltie reported the many conjectures that had been heard at the senior center, and Gracie got wind of still others as she talked to friends around town.

Tom Ritter and his wife went off on an extended Caribbean cruise, which rather surprised Uncle Miltie, who stated that if he were mayor and had only a couple of months left in his term, he'd stick around and try to do at least something to show how indispensable he was.

After church one Sunday morning, Rocky joined Gracie and her uncle at the deli, and were greeted by Abe with, "Welcome, my friends! There's someone waiting here to see you."

As they headed back to the corner table, Gracie said, "We missed you at church, Davena."

"I missed going, too," she stated, indicating with a hand motion that they should join her. "I was tied up all night long having major problems with a litter of puppies."

"Are they okay?"

She looked tired but pleased, the way a skilled professional does after a job well done. "The first one died, but the rest seem to be doing fairly well now. Still, it was touch-and-go for a while."

Rocky asked, "Are they registered?"

She shook her head. "No, but they're loved."

"And that makes them even more valuable," Gracie affirmed.

They gave their orders, and it was when Abe was delivering their food that he mentioned, "Tony was in last evening. . ."

"How's he doing, after getting so few votes?"

He sighed. "I feel sort of sorry for the guy, Gracie. I get the idea he'd been led to believe all those rumors he was hearing about Elmo, and regrets having helped to spread them. If that's the case, I can sort of see why he agreed to run."

"Oh?"

"I believe Harvey was sure that since he's a very successful businessman in town, he could attract a fair number of votes—but figured this time that having another name in the pot would dilute the number of votes for Tom, and also those you'd get, Gracie."

She shook her head. "It's still a puzzlement to me why so many people thought I'd be eager to run."

"Because you didn't come right out and say you wouldn't," Rocky reminded her. "But I'm glad you've remained in private life."

"Me, too!" She took a bite of her toasted bagel. "And I think Elmo, watching over me, has got to be relieved. As dedicated as he was himself, he'd have understood my reluctance to be forced to run."

"Okay," Rocky teased, "so being mayor of Willow Bend is out. But what if you truly were called to some higher office? President Gracie Parks, for instance?"

"I'd have to decide whether to make Uncle Miltie 'First Uncle' or else put him in charge of the Pun-tagon."

"Oh, Gracie," said Rocky, "you really have had him around too long!"

"Praise the Lord!" said Uncle Miltie. "I'll vote for that!"

RECIPE

Gracie's Plum Cake

- ✓ 2 cups flour
- ✓ 1 stick of butter or margarine
- ✓ 1 egg
- ✓ 2 tablespoons of cream or milk
- ✓ Sugar
- ✓ Cinnamon
- ✓ 12–14 Italian prune plums or purple plums
- ✓ Extra pat of butter, cut up into small pieces

Cut the stick of butter into the flour until small crumbs appear. Gently mix in egg and milk until a dough is formed. Pat the dough into a thin layer on the bottom of an oblong baking dish, making sure there's a small edge. Split the plums and set them in rows into the dough. Sprinkle them with sugar and cinnamon, and then dot the tops of the plums with butter. Bake in a 350-degree oven until the dough is golden-brown and the fruit is well-cooked.

Gracie says, "This is a simple, delicious recipe—similar to Abe's plum *kuchen*—that I got from Aunt Doris, Uncle Miltie's wife. It can be varied with the addition of other fruit. For example, plums go well with peaches or cherries. Sometimes I put the tiniest smidgeon of orange marmalade into the center of each plum before adding the sugar, cinnamon and butter, which really makes for an unexpected and yummy taste sensation."

About the Author

EILEEN M. BERGER always loved to read and promised herself as a child to someday write books. Her degrees, however, from Bucknell and Temple universities, were in biology, chemistry and medical technology, which led to her becoming head of a large pathology laboratory. And after falling in love with Bob, whom she'd known since she was five years old, Eileen became the wife of a pastor in north-central Pennsylvania.

With the advent of three little ones—and with fifteen other children on the block apparently thinking they lived at the parsonage, except for being sent home for meals and bedtime—Eileen at first wrote and sold only short articles, poems and children's stories.

As the children got older, Eileen substituted as a teacher in Hughesville High School and worked part-time in the laboratories of the community hospital. This latter job became full-time when Bob and Eileen bought the property outside of town, where they still live. They grow choose-and-cut Christmas trees on part of this land and on their farm sixteen miles away.

Eileen's first five novels, written on the small portable typewriter kept on the dining room table, were still unsold when number six was accepted for publication—and two more books were contracted for within the next thirteen months. Twelve more have followed, along with hundreds of short stories, novellas, articles and prayers.

Eileen began writing full-time following a serious accident, and continues to teach in workshops, schools and conferences. She's active in the West Branch Christian Writers, which she helped found twenty-some years ago, is a long-time board member of St. Davids Christian Writers Association and with Pennwriters. Without these wonderful, dedicated people and their invaluable yearly conferences, Eileen says she might still be a struggling wanna-be writer.